Judicial Homicide

Tales of Executions

JUDICIAL HOMICIDE – TALES OF EXECUTIONS

Cover Design By James, GoOnWrite.com

Editing: D.L. Winchester

First edition 2024

Contents

Introduction

By D.L. Winchester (Editor)

When I put out a call for an anthology, I try not to limit myself to a specific "vision" for how the anthology will turn out. My first priority is to find great stories (the long list), then find stories that work well with each other (the short list) to make a final anthology that is enjoyable and entertaining for you, the reader.

Sometimes, this is easy. Other times, not so much.

Judicial Homicide turned out to be one of the other times.

For a while, I was worried about getting enough submissions to have an anthology. We got there in the end, but my long list turned out to be, well, not very long at all. But the stories that made the long list were fantastic. This anthology was probably the most difficult to cut down to the final table of contents. Every story in the long list was fantastic, and could have made the short list and the final cut. It took some gnashing of teeth, but I finally made my picks.

Then I looked at the cover I'd purchased, and realized we didn't have a story that focused on hanging as a method of execution. The great Rebecca Cuthbert stepped in and offered to write a poem, bailing me out on that front.

After that, things smoothed out. Thankfully.

And the final anthology is awesome.

I've been interested in the death penalty for as long as I can remember, so it was an easy decision to build an anthology around it. Even easier was the decision to make it a charity anthology in support of Witness to Innocence, an organization supporting exonerated death row inmates.

Interestingly, I discovered Witness to Innocence through a post in a community Facebook group. Ray Krone, the 100th person to be exonerated following the resumption of Capital Punishment in 1976 and a co-founder of Witness to Innocence, moved to Tennessee and is in a relationship with a writer. When his partner posted about her book signing, I pulled up her profile to see if I knew her and what she wrote. She had Witness to Innocence on her page, I was curious, and soon, I was reading *Jingle Jangle: The Perfect Crime Turned Inside Out*, Jim Rix's excellent telling of the events surrounding Ray's conviction and exoneration.

After I finished *Jingle Jangle* and learned more about Witness to Innocence, the ideas started to merge: execution-themed anthology and charity donation in one. Soon, it was on the Undertaker Books calendar, and now it's in your hands to enjoy.

So here you are, dear reader. Ten stories of judicial homicide, death delivered for a purpose, real or imagined. I hope you enjoy this anthology as much as I've enjoyed putting it together.

D.L. Winchester
September 5, 2024
Newport, TN

A Curse Thrown from the Old Hanging Tree

Rebecca Cuthbert

A fledgling town near an old craggy shore
is the setting of this woeful tale—
a story of need and of lies and of greed
and a hanging that more or less failed.

This town had a church that was led by a man
who on Sundays would preach against sin,
but by Tuesday nights with his breeches too tight
he would seek sweet relief at an inn.

The woman he met there had dark roving eyes
and a mouth like a ripe peach just plucked—
a young widow herself, with no means and no wealth,
she would charge a gold coin to be fucked.

The preacher would pay, sometimes twice before dawn,
glad to revel in pleasures she offered,
and what did he care, since the pricey affair
was afforded by skimming church coffers?

For months this continued in shadowy secret;
the widow had pledged her discretion—
but one hot June night in revealing moonlight
her round belly foretold her confession.

"Forgive me, my lord," said the woman through tears,
"but I promise, you're my only lover."
The preacher's mind raced, color blanched from his face;
he'd be ruined with this truth uncovered.

"There's more," wept the woman, "for my sister knows
and demanded I tell her who'd bed me,
she ran to our mother, who then told my brother,
and he'll importune that you wed me."

Ignoring her pleas, he stormed out of the inn,
how *dare* she give him so little warning?

All week rumors flew and the whispers did too—
the town knew his shame by Sunday morning.

So "Harlot!" he cried, and then "Heathen!" and "Whore!"
and "Black witchcraft!" he blamed for his lusting;
the parish was shocked but he promised his flock
he was still the man they could put trust in.

"We can't let her live!" he declared from his pulpit,
"I'll lead tonight's posse to get her!
A *witch* in our midst," he screamed, shaking his fist,
"will corrupt every man if we let her!"

So torches were lighted and pitchforks were gathered,
and mercy abandoned for malice.
Soon, gagged and bound, she was carried through town
by a mob both bloodthirsty and callous.

They surged north and east to an infamous hill
that the local kids swore was long haunted,
and though her family cried they were all pushed aside
for a hanging was what the mob wanted.

On that hill an oak stood called "The Old Hanging Tree"
and the doomed widow saw what awaited—
but she also knew the witchcraft charge was *true*
  and revenge is best when it's belated.

Her preacher ex-lover removed the rough gag
and said "Here is your last chance to pray."
"Fool!" the witch jeered, "I'll be back in a year
and it's more than a gold coin you'll pay!"

There in the gloaming he pulled the noose tight
with her words ringing loud in his ears,
then six men yanked her high into that purple sky
and the hillside resounded with cheers.

Her neck didn't break, though it should have been quick;
"No matter!" he called, "let her strangle!"
They waited a while, stared at her frozen smile,
but then ran when she laughed as she dangled.

The preacher fled fastest and flew to his church
to prostrate himself there on God's altar,

but it was no use; He would broker no truce,
and the preacher had no way to halt her.

He knew she'd return and in twelve months she did,
one late night as he lay barely sleeping.
He woke with a cry, pinned between her strong thighs,
and her moans almost drowned out his weeping.

"I'm almost there, preacher," she whimpered and writhed,
and she rocked her hips harder and faster,
then she grabbed his throat and she squeezed til he choked
as they sped toward climax and disaster.

"Come for me, preacher!" she yelled and he did,
though his vision had already faded,
he left this world shamed as someone called his name—
not the witch, but the devil who waited.

Rebecca Cuthbert writes dark fiction and poetry. Her books
include In Memory of Exoskeletons (Alien Buddha Press),

Creep This Way: How to Become a Horror Writer with 24 Tips to Get You Ghouling (Seamus & Nunzio Productions), and the forthcoming Self-Made Monsters (ABP) and The Hauntings Back Home (Undertaker Books). She comes to Undertaker with an MFA in Fiction from West Virginia University and an extensive background in editing and teaching. Some of her favorite subgenres and aesthetics are feminist horror, gothic thrillers, the Grotesque, slipstream, dark fairy tales, eco horror, and ghost stories.

A Boating Judge

Kay Hanifen

The problem with executions, Judge Wharton had decided, was they were too humane. All anyone ever cared about was the murderer and their suffering.

But what about the victims?

Where was the justice in a quick death?

The families of the victims would have to live the rest of their lives with what happened weighing on their souls, but the killer would experience their release from life in a swift and timely manner, courtesy of the eighth amendment.

But sometimes, people deserve cruel and unusual punishments.

Case in point: Wesley Rogers. He was scum, pure and simple. Over the course of a year, he murdered four teenage boys. Judge Wharton was certain of it. But the jury was not convinced. The bleeding hearts heard his story—how mental illness led to homelessness, and how he stumbled onto the body of Gregory Pierce while looking for shelter one winter day—and they believed him. Sure, most of the evidence was circumstantial, but Judge Wharton could tell just by looking at him that he was the killer of those four boys.

He hated that he had to let Wesley go, but he knew it wouldn't be for long. Judge Wharton and the local sheriff, Sheriff Eliot, had a certain arrangement when it came to scum like this.

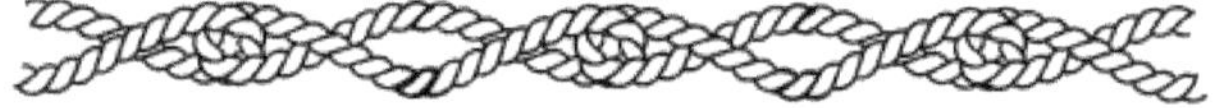

As he waited on the front porch of his hunting lodge, he could see the police cruiser pulling into the long driveway. It was a shame the justice system failed, but he and the sheriff were there to fill in for its shortcomings.

When the sheriff brought his car to a stop, he opened the door and dragged a wide-eyed Wesley out of the vehicle. He was a hulking man, nearly six-foot-five, with broad shoulders and massive hands, hands made to be wrapped around the throats of teenage boys. He had trimmed his beard for his court date, a far cry from the scraggly woodsman the police had booked in county jail.

Wesley blinked in confusion as he glanced around the hunting lodge. "Where am I?" he asked in his usual whisper. Judge Wharton had been shocked when he first heard Wesley speak. For such a big man, he was soft spoken. It seemed wrong. His voice should have been booming enough to fill the courtroom.

So, it had to be an act.

His lawyers instructed him to speak softly to make him seem less threatening, but if anything, it added to his inherent wrongness.

Because there was something wrong with him. Only a twisted soul would murder four innocent kids.

"Welcome," Judge Wharton said.

Wesley's attention snapped to him, his brows furrowing in confusion. "Your Honor?"

Judge Wharton smiled. "You don't have to be so formal. We aren't in the courtroom right now. Just call me Judge or sir."

"Y-yes, sir." Licking his dry lips, Wesley glanced around. "I thought I was going to be released to a group home. Where am I?"

"You're at my hunting lodge."

He swallowed, his Adam's apple bobbing. He looked like a cornered deer, ready to bolt. "I don't understand."

"Come on now," Sheriff Eliot said, throwing his arm around Wesley's shoulder in a mock show of friendliness. But his grip was tight, making any potential escape difficult. "We both know why you're here. What you did…"

"I didn't—"

"It's pointless to lie now," Wharton cut in. "We all know the truth."

Wesley shook his head. "I'm innocent. The jury said so."

"You can fool a jury, but you can't fool me, son." Mood abruptly changing, he clapped his hands and smiled genially. "Now, what do you want for dinner? I can whip up just about anything you'd like."

"What?"

"For your last meal." He turned and opened the door to the lodge. Wesley froze, his breath coming out in short pants as his wide eyes darted around, searching for a means of escape.

"Come on." Eliot growled, giving him a shove forward. The sheriff entered, his arm still around Wesley's shoulders, gripping him in case he tried to run. Wharton followed close behind.

Eliot sat Wesley down at the kitchen table. The judge followed the prisoner's gaze out the window to the boat floating on the lake. It was a unique contraption, more like a coffin on water than a rowboat. The bottom portion was a regular canoe, but the top had a hinge and a roof. There were five holes. The largest sat at the end of the canoe. Two parallel holes had been carved near it while the other two had been carved near the bottom.

"What's that?" Wesley asked, his voice shaky.

"Don't worry about it just yet. Let's focus on dinner. What can I make you?"

"Duck confit," he replied, much to the surprise of the judge. Wesley struck him as more of a fast-food guy.

He arched an eyebrow. "You have a refined palate."

Wesley didn't take his eyes off the boat. "I was a chef before...before I was on the streets. It was my favorite dish to make."

"You learn something new every day." With his hands behind his back, he wandered to the mantle, where he kept his father's rifle, a vintage M-1 Garand. The late judge started his career as a military executioner, using the rifle to execute war criminals and spies during the Second World War. Wharton considered it his prized possession.

Taking the rifle, he checked that it was loaded. It always was, but it still didn't hurt to make sure. Satisfied, he headed back to the kitchen with the gun in hand. "Sheriff, if you don't mind running to the grocery store, I wasn't expecting to make a confit."

The sheriff gave him a quizzical look, but still nodded in acquiescence.

Wharton could see what Wesley was doing. It was obvious he picked a time-consuming recipe so that he could plan his escape. The judge had seen several of his condemned try it, and all had failed. But it wouldn't hurt to humor the man a bit before dashing his hopes.

Eliot pulled out his handcuffs. "Take that chair next to the metal ring in the wall there."

Wesley glared at him but did as he asked, letting the sheriff handcuff him to the ring.

"One wrong move and the judge will blow your brains out. Understood?"

"Yeah."

"What was that?" The sheriff's jaw tightened.

"Yes...sir." The words dripped with venom, but both judge and sheriff chose to ignore it.

"That's right." With that, he left to pick up the items for Wesley's menu.

"What are you going to do to me?" Wesley asked, his gaze burning a hole into the floor.

Judge Wharton arched an eyebrow. "Are you sure you want to know?"

He still didn't meet the judge's gaze. "Yeah."

"Gregory Pierce, Keenan Smith, William Patterson, and Joseph Archer. Were their deaths quick?"

"You tell me. I'm not the one who did it."

The judge rolled his eyes. "Are you really going to keep up this charade?"

The only response was Wesley's sullen silence. Judge Wharton expected nothing less.

"I'm a student of history. Did you know that?"

He shook his head, still not speaking.

"The ancients knew how to get rid of criminals and deter anyone else considering a life of crime." Judge Wharton smiled as he stared out the window, watching the boat bobbing gently on the water. "They were as cruel as they were creative. Personally, I've always been fond of the Bronze Bull. That was a hollow metal statue. They'd place the victim inside and light a fire underneath it. The prisoner would slowly roast alive, their screams warping and emanating from the bull's mouth like the bellowing of a living animal."

Wesley's head shot up at that. He looked vaguely nauseous. "And you want to do that to me?"

The judge sighed. "Unfortunately, a bespoke bronze bull statue is outside my pay grade and far too suspicious. No, my execution method of choice is the boats out there. They call it scaphism, from the Greek word meaning 'to hollow.' You'll learn why it's called that soon enough."

He bit back a smile at the memory of the last execution he had conducted. The condemned was a man named Tom Wilson, a scumbag who raped and murdered his girlfriend, only to be freed on a technicality. Like Wesley, he maintained his innocence until the end.

Tom Wilson decided to forego his last meal, yelling obscenities at the judge and sheriff until the sheriff punched him out. The two men carried the condemned to the boats and secured him while he was unconscious. In ancient times, they force fed the condemned milk and honey to make them defecate themselves before smearing it all over the exposed parts of their bodies. The two honored that tradition by using milk and honey on the arms, legs, and face, but to make him go, they force-fed him laxatives.

Then, they set him adrift. For days, the condemned screamed while insects buzzed around his head and burrowed into him, devouring him from the inside out. To keep him alive, they pulled him to shore once a day to make him drink water and force feed him whatever they had on hand. Then, more laxatives.

Tom Wilson lasted for two weeks. The sheriff and Eliot had to wear masks when they pulled him to shore for the last time. Insects still buzzed around his sunburned face, the burns so severe that the skin looked leathery in places and had bubbled and blistered in others. A second- and third-degree burn. These burns covered all exposed skin, but the real horror show was when they opened the top boat.

The odor was horrific. Excrement and urine mixed with blood. A swarm of flies, freed by the opening of the top, buzzed away, revealing rancid flesh in the process of being eaten by writhing maggots. Though he'd been through this several times before, the reveal never failed to make Wharton gag.

He and Eliot punctured the lungs to prevent flotation and make sure he was dead before dumping the body in the lake to become fish food. Then, they used a power wash to rinse out the boat for its next use.

"So, you're gonna trap me in those boats?" Wesley asked, snapping the judge out of his reverie. "And what? I'll die of dehydration?"

"Something like that," he replied. There was a fine line between instilling an appropriate amount of fear and making sure Wesley wouldn't try to escape until it was too late. After all, he was much bigger than his captors. It wouldn't take much for him to wrestle away the gun and shoot them both.

"Why are you so convinced I killed those boys?" he asked, his voice so soft that it was barely audible.

The judge blinked. This wasn't a question that most of his condemned asked, mainly because they already knew the answer. Judge Wharton saw right through them and needed to ensure that they would never harm anyone again. Instead, they usually just insisted upon their innocence, no matter how dubious it may be.

But Wesley was staring at him as though he was waiting for an answer. The judge scoffed. "I listened to the evidence and came to my own conclusion. You may have fooled the jury, but you didn't fool me. I see what you are."

"A crazy, homeless man. A perfect scapegoat while the real killer is free to keep on murdering," Wesley replied. He didn't look angry. Simply resigned. "They tried to push me into making a plea deal. My own lawyers told me I should take it because no jury would believe me. But I wasn't about to take the fall for something I didn't do. It wasn't right. And guess what? I won. So, with all that stacked against me, what does that say about my guilt?"

"That the jury is a bunch of bleeding hearts." Judge Wharton sat back in his chair, crossing his legs, as though they were chatting over cigars rather than preparing for an execution. "They heard a sob story and decided a piece of shit like you deserved to live when those poor families had to bury their children."

"Really? You're convinced of my guilt beyond any reasonable doubt?"

"None whatsoever."

He sighed. "Well, I guess that's it, then. But can I have my meds? They keep me level. I'd like to die with dignity."

"I can't promise dignity," the judge replied. "But I'll give you your medications. Where are they?"

"In the sheriff's car with the rest of my things from jail."

Judge Wharton checked the window. Sheriff Eliot had taken the judge's car, meaning the police vehicle was still sitting there. "Fine. But don't try anything. I might decide to revoke your last meal privileges and proceed with the execution."

Wesley shrugged. "I don't think I can go anywhere anyway."

The judge eyed him suspiciously but headed out the door. He was quick, but not quick enough. The moment he stepped back through the door, he heard a crack and a yell.

Wesley stood there, panting, his wrists still bound and bleeding from where the metal handcuffs bit into them, the ring hanging between them on the chain. The brick wall had a spiderweb of cracks where he pulled it out in a feat of desperate strength. For a moment, the judge gaped. But then he remembered that he had a rifle in his hands. Dropping the medication, he shouldered the gun and took aim.

Wesley leapt, taking cover behind the wall as brick exploded into powder where he once stood. "I didn't kill them," he shouted.

"I don't care." The judge moved slowly, rounding the corner with the barrel of the gun leading. "You're still a drain on society. The world would be better off without shit like you."

"Finally, you're telling the truth," Wesley replied. His massive hands shot out and grabbed the barrel of the gun. They wrestled, but the judge was not a young man anymore. Wesley had the dual advantages of youth and strength. The judge pulled the trigger twice, the bullets exploding from the gun like claps of thunder and lodging in walls.

But Wesley wrenched it free. He turned the weapon and struck the judge with the barrel. Wharton saw stars, his knees collapsing under him as a wave of nausea threatened to carry his lunch to shore. There were hands patting him down and a frantic muttering of, "Keys, keys, keys."

But the sheriff had them, not the judge, meaning Wesley wasn't getting out of his cuffs any time soon. Despite the burst of pain in his head, Judge Wharton laughed to himself at that realization.

He stopped laughing when he realized that the gun was pointed at his forehead.

"How many?" Wesley demanded. "How many have you killed?"

"Five men. All guilty as sin." The judge was many things, but he refused to be a coward, even in the face of death.

"Where are the bodies?"

"In the lake, nothing but bones. They weren't recognizable as anything human once we were done with them."

"You're a monster," Wesley growled.

"I fight monsters."

His finger hovered over the trigger. "Is there a difference?"

The judge chuckled. "How very Nietzschean of you. So, now that you have me where you want me, are you going to kill me and prove me right?" It was a gamble to challenge him, but if he was as innocent as he claimed, then he would not be able to stomach the idea of committing murder in cold blood.

Wesley hesitated, his Adam's apple bobbing as he swallowed. "I'll forget about this," he said, nervously licking his lips. "I'll leave town. You and the sheriff will never see me again."

Judge Wharton was about to agree, just to buy time if nothing else, but then the door swung open. "I'm back," Eliot called as he stepped inside. When he spotted Wesley holding the gun, his eyes widened. "Shit!" he exclaimed, then reached for his gun.

Wesley was faster. He took aim and fired, hitting the sheriff in the chest. *But he did not shoot the deputy*, the judge thought.

Eliot hit the ground with a dull thud, blood pooling beneath him. Wesley stared in wide-eyed horror. "Oh God," he whispered.

"See? You're a killer," the judge said.

"Shut up!" Wesley aimed a kick to the judge's head, knocking him back to the ground. He ran over to Eliot and dug through his pockets until he found the keys to the handcuffs.

Judge Wharton watched through half-lidded eyes and double vision as Wesley fumbled with the lock for a few moments before freeing one wrist, and then the other. Then, the world faded to black.

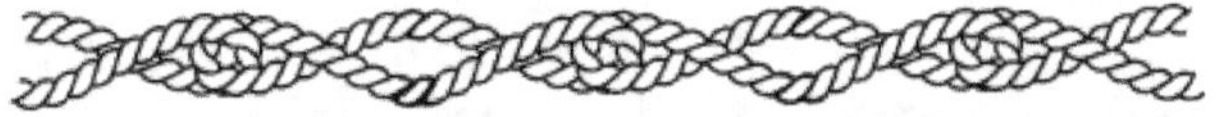

He woke to something sticky and wet on top of him. It was heavy, making it difficult to move, and it smelled of aftershave and cigarettes. And on top of that was the odor of blood. Wharton's stomach churned when the reality of his situation finally hit him.

The sheriff's corpse was lying across his chest.

One of the judge's hands had been handcuffed to the body while the other was trapped somehow. Immobile.

He could feel a familiar shifting underneath him. The gentle rocking of a boat on water. And then he realized where he was.

"It only seemed fair that you would get to find out what it's like," Wesley said. "It's like the song says: 'Let the punishment fit the crime.'"

A bolt of panic coursed through him. "No, no, please," Judge Wharton begged. "I did it all for the good of humanity."

"I don't care," Wesley replied. "You're still a drain on society. The world would be better off without shit like you." With that, he pushed the boat away from the dock.

Judge Wharton was set adrift, screaming for mercy.

Kay Hanifen was born on a Friday the 13th and once lived for three months in a haunted castle. So, obviously, she had to become a horror writer. Her work has appeared in over forty anthologies and magazines. When she's not consuming pop culture with the voraciousness of a vampire at a 24-hour blood bank, you can usually find her with two black cats or at kayhanifenauthor.wordpress.com.

Twelve Good Men And True

Rosetta Yorke

Icy water drenched Jed's darkness with the slimy stink of shit. He spluttered back to consciousness and rough, sodden burlap smothering his face. A wooden bucket thudded onto the floor next to him, the hollow sound echoing. It died away into a squeaky scuffling noise that made his head throb. His mouth tasted of stale vomit. He lay huddled on his side, the stone beneath him so cold his limbs had seized solid. Rope tying his arms behind his back gouged his wrists. His coat was missing. His body felt like it had been pummeled.

Hands hauled him up and shoved him onto a stool low and narrow enough for his buttocks to sag off either side of it. Someone yanked the sack off his head. A man spoke, but the background squeaking distorted his words. Jed prised his gummy eyelids open. He peered through the flickering candlelight at a group of shadowy figures seated around three sides of a short stone table.

"Where am I?" he croaked. His gaze bounced to the thin lancet window behind them, black as the night outside, and he knew—the crypt beneath St. Mary's. He swayed, hairs prickling on his arms. That wasn't a table, it was an altar. "What's happening? Why am I here?" The last thing he remembered was giving Blaze a nosebag while his rabbit stew supper simmered over his campfire in the clearing.

The central figure leaned forward into the candlelight. He propped his elbows on the stone and steepled his fingers. "Jed Suggitt, you are accused of carrying out unspeakable crimes. How do you plead?"

Jed recognised him as Ralph Langthorne, the squire's son. He didn't know the other men, but ale-gossip in the Langthorne Arms of late had been of him and his rich London friends kicking up larks all over the parish. They'd gone too far this time, roughing him up and disrespecting St. Mary's. But, at least, they were gentlemen. Likely they'd compensate him for his injuries, and Father Corden for any damage to the crypt. "What crimes might those be, sir?"

"Abducting my fiancée, Miss Sarah Elgin, as she took the air in the Manor's parterre. Forcing yourself upon her in the vilest fashion—"

"What?" Heat flooded Jed's face and neck. "No! For shame, Master Ralph! You shouldn't make sport out of a lady's reputation." His voice's high pitch hurt his head.

"Sport?" Langthorne's fist smashed down on the altar, making Jed flinch and the squeaking intensify. "Is that what you call pursuing her when she fled, screaming for her life, through Langthorne Woods?"

A jagged memory flashed into Jed's mind like a lightning bolt forking across a thunder-charred sky.

The undergrowth rustles. Blaze snorts and flattens his ears. A dark-haired woman bursts through the trees, her eyes wide and white circled, her dress all dirty, bloody and torn, her exposed breasts purpled with finger-marks—he didn't want to think about those, it wasn't proper.

"She wasn't screaming," he said. "She didn't make a sound." Shock, or terror, must have tied her tongue. There had been a scream, though, later. He fumbled through his groggy mind, but the why and when of it eluded him.

"How could she, by the time you'd finished with her?" The dark-haired man next to Langthorne spoke in an even tone, but his fingers twisted his coat cuff until the button flew off and pinged across the altar like a pebble skimming a stagnant pond. The man slapped his hand down and flattened it. "My sister was dead. You'd murdered her."

"Dead?" She couldn't be. Jed swallowed rapidly. "How?"

"Stabbed through the heart. By you."

"I never touched her—I wouldn't." They couldn't think it was him. Was any of this even true? But it didn't feel much like a game.

"Your clothes condemn you."

He looked down. Pain jabbed his neck muscles. Dark splotches—not from skinning the rabbit—stained his flannel shirt.

The woman stumbles toward him. "Help me!" she begs. She clutches his lapels and clings to him. She reeks of musk and urine like from a rutting goat, but the faintest hint of wild jasmine lingers at her throat.

"She was still alive when I saw her," he said.

"But not when you left her." The woman's brother produced a knife and brandished it at him across the altar. "Is this yours?"

Jed peered through the shadows. "Can't be. That blade's all messy. I'd never leave mine in that state."

"What did you have for your supper?" Langthorne asked.

Why did he want to know? "Rabbit stew, not that I've had it yet. It's probably burnt by now, unless you put my fire out?"

"Maybe something distracted you? Maybe you forget to clean your knife after preparing your meal?"

Jed scowled. He had his pride. "No," he insisted. "After I'd skinned and jointed the rabbit, I wiped my knife on the grass and put it away in my coat pocket. I remember doing that. There wasn't a spot of blood left on its blade." To clinch the matter, he added, "Mine has a bone handle with my initials carved into it."

"Show him the knife, Elgin," Langthorne said.

The woman's brother handed the knife to the man next to him who examined it and passed it on. Jed watched the knife travel from hand to hand, scrutiny to scrutiny, around the altar. He watched their expressions change, their eyes narrow and their mouths pinch—a murder of crows gathering in judgement of him. Sweat beaded his forehead. How many of them were there? He counted: four men to the left of Langthorne and four, including Elgin, to his right. Jed closed his eyes for a long moment and slowly exhaled. *Only nine.* Not enough for a trial jury, even if this felt like one. Anyway, folks were always innocent until proven guilty and they couldn't do that because he wasn't.

Footsteps clumped past him from behind. He snapped his eyes open. A giant of a man in a leather apron strode to the altar. What was Bennet doing here? But thank goodness he was. Jed could rely on the blacksmith for help. They'd done business together over a mug of ale for years. He always sold his scrap metal pickings on to Bennet, and Bennet made good profits from reusing them. He was the nearest Jed had to a friend.

Bennet left the altar and clumped back toward him. He thrust his hand out flat, level with Jed's nose. His calloused palm was huge, fleshy and mottled as a Dryad's Saddle mushroom. Across his furrowed lifeline lay a bloodstained knife with *J.S.* carved into its bone handle.

His initials. *His* knife. Too late Jed recognized the trap his own pride had sprung.

He shook his head. "I didn't do it." He looked into Bennet's face and met only a cold, hard stare and a curled lip in response. "You know me, Bennet." His voice rose. "You know I'd never—"

Bennet turned on his heel and walked away. He placed the pocketknife on the altar in front of Langthorne and took up a position standing behind him.

Jed sagged. His vision blurred. If Bennet didn't believe him, who would? *Ten men.*

"The evidence against you speaks for itself, Suggitt. We found you in Langthorne Woods next to Miss Elgin's body." Langthorne placed a comforting hand on Elgin's shoulder. "Your shirt is stained with Miss Elgin's blood, as is your knife—it can't be animal blood because you're adamant you cleaned the blade thoroughly after preparing your supper."

"Where's his coat?" Elgin asked. "He said he'd put the knife in its pocket."

"He didn't have one when we found him," Langthorne said.

Bennet cleared his throat. "His coat's black, sir. He always wears the same one. I've never seen him without it before today." His gaze flicked to Jed and shied away again. "Perhaps it's in his pack."

"Bring it here," Langthorne said.

Bennet strode past Jed. The clump-clump of his boots tolled in Jed's ears with the finality of a Passing Bell.

When Bennet reappeared, he carried Jed's pack over his shoulder. At a gesture from Langthorne, he loosened its cord and emptied the contents out onto the floor in front of the altar. Woollen rags, rabbit and cat skins, holed stockings, a threadbare blanket, and second-hand clothes tumbled into a heap. Bennet rummaged through them, lifting each item up in turn for the men to view. A spotted neckerchief tore in his hands.

"That's my livelihood," Jed protested.

"How is that possible?" sneered a man on the left. "Who'd buy such things?"

"Rags go for paper, bones for cutlery handles, and I suppose the poor can't afford new clothes," Langthorne said.

The man flushed. "My household's cutlery has ivory handles."

"There!" Elgin pointed.

Bennet yanked a black frock coat out by its sleeve and deposited it on the altar. The crows examined it.

"That's not mine," Jed said. "I've never seen it before."

"The front panel has a large damp patch." Langthorne brought the fabric up to his nose and sniffed. "Blood."

"If it's not your coat, Suggitt, where did it come from?" Elgin asked.

Jed sat straighter, wincing when he moved too sharply. "I'm a rag-and-bone man, sir. I collect old clothes." He licked his lips. "I called at the Manor late this afternoon. The footman gave me some of the servants' cast-offs. Maybe it was amongst those." But he knew it hadn't been.

"The cloth's too fine for a servant to wear," Elgin's neighbour objected.

"I pass my last-season's attire on to my valet," someone else said. "He's a good man. Deserves a reward now and then—"

"Did you encounter Miss Elgin while you were at the Manor?" Langthorne said.

"No."

"I think you did. I think you saw her, and lusted after her. I think you put this coat on to impress her—"

"I didn't see no one." Spots danced in front of Jed's eyes.

"You hid, waiting your chance to catch her on her own. You accosted her. You abducted her. You forced yourself on her in the woods. You brutally murdered her to conceal your crimes." Langthorne's spittle splattered the altar. "You hid the coat among—"

"I didn't."

The woman says something over and over, but he loses the words in her softness and her bruises and the tears on her face. The scent of jasmine burns in him like fever. "You're safe now," he says. His chest flutters with his need to help her. She looks over his shoulder and screams. He senses movement behind him. She screams again.

"It wasn't me!" Jed cried. "Someone else was there too."

"Who?"

"I didn't see him. He came up behind me. That's all I remember. He must have hit me over the head, knocked me senseless."

"And after he'd killed her, I suppose he swapped his coat for yours to make his escape?"

"Yes." Jed darted a glance at Bennet who was still rummaging about on the floor. What was he up to? He'd already discovered the coat. What else did he expect to find amongst Jed's pickings?

With an *aha*-flourish, Bennet produced a knotted fold of dark cloth and laid it on the altar. Langthorne seized it, teased the knot undone and unfolded the cloth.

Elgin pounced on the glittering contents. "My sister's earrings, blood-stained where you tore them from her ears, you fiend!" he howled. Leaping up, he hurtled toward Jed.

Jed tried to rise, but his legs wobbled, and he tipped backward off the stool. The crypt spiralled around him. He crashed onto the floor and lay there, his chest heaving for air. Hands closed around his neck, throttling him. He writhed, but with bound hands he couldn't break the unrelenting grip. Pinpricks of light sparkled. His ears popped.

Voices boomed. He dragged agonizing breath into his lungs. After a while, he realized the pressure on his throat had eased. A cold stone wall propped up his back. Discordant voices rose and fell. They battered him until, finally, their differences smoothed into a harmonious whole that let him drift toward oblivion.

Footsteps clumped, growing louder. Bennet hauled him up and manhandled him across to the altar. He sagged onto the stool. Bennet wrenched him up again.

"Stand up, Suggitt," Langthorne said. "The evidence against you is unequivocal. You've provided us with no alibi, no defense, no remorse for your despicable crimes. For the brutal rape and murder of Miss Elgin, we find you—"

"Guilty!" chorused the others.

"—Guilty!" Langthorne declared.

Guilty, guilty, guilty. It echoed in the walls and the roof and the floor. The crypt constricted around him, crushing him with the weight of the word. *Guilty.*

He fought to dig himself free. "I didn't do it." His voice rasped. His swollen lips cracked with the metallic tang of blood. "Not a jury. Not enough."

"There's nine of us," said Elgin. "The blacksmith makes ten." He paused, waiting.

Bennet's response plummeted through the silence. "Guilty!"

"Megson?" Langthorne prompted.

"Guilty!" came a reedy voice from the back of the crypt.

The ratcatcher? What was he doing here? "Of course, you'd say that, you weasel-faced backstabber!" Jed shouted. "You've been trying to poach my business for the last two years." But his words lost their way in the grayness clamping his head in an ever-tightening band and only garbled groans emerged from his inflamed throat. No one heeded them.

"Eleven men," Elgin said. "And Lord Langthorne, when he arrives, makes twelve. That's a full complement for you, Suggitt."

"My father's verdict from the outset has been 'Guilty.'"

"Then we're unanimous," Elgin said. "I want justice for my sister. Let his punishment fit his crime."

At a gesture from Langthorne, Bennet seized Jed's arms and hauled him away into the centre of the crypt. He threw him down as if he were a sack of coal.

Jed's back smacked the floor. Shooting pain skewered his spine. His bound wrists cracked beneath him. His head thumped onto stone.

The woman says something, but her jasmine softness muffles it.

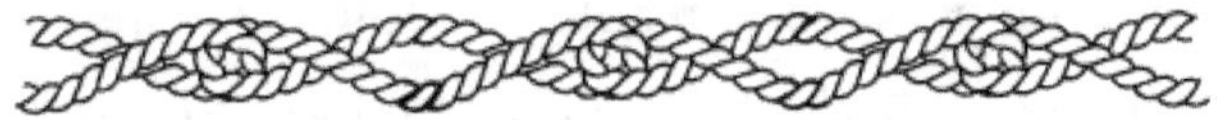

Fragmented sounds pierced the darkness cocooning him. Megson's shrill voice cried, "You can't. I'll have no part of it!"

"You agreed to provide us with—" came Langthorne's curt reply.

"I didn't know *that's* why you wanted—I won't—"

"Then go. But leave those. They're ours, bought and paid for by my father."

"I don't want the money. Take it back."

Noises of a violent struggle followed. Coins rang out in a fusillade of chinks against stone. Hasty footsteps retreated up the staircase. A distant door thudded shut.

The woman's face hovers in front of him. Her lips move. Her tear-filled eyes implore him to listen.

Her urgent insistence jolted Jed out of drifting into nothingness. He crawled through the cavernous nightmares in his mind, dredging their horrors until he discovered what she'd said. With a flurry of hope, he groped his way back up to the surface, but as consciousness returned, so did agonizing pain. Its shards racked his body, obliterating the woman's words and, with them, his one chance to save himself.

He couldn't move. He lay stripped naked and spreadeagled. Ropes bound his wrists and ankles to four iron rings set into the crypt's freezing flagstone floor. Livid welts and bruises purpled his chest.

Bennet appeared carrying a shallow, bottomless metal box. He strapped it over Jed's belly and buckled it tight until its sharp side-edges dug deep into his flesh. Bennet tugged on the box, checking it couldn't move. He slid a bolt back on the top and opened a flap.

The crows clustered around Jed, looming over him, with the squire in their midst now, too. Ralph Langthorne held out the bloodstained pocketknife. Elgin took it.

"I didn't—" Jed protested.

"For my sister," Elgin said. He inserted the knife into the box and slashed its blade across Jed's belly. He handed the knife to Langthorne.

"Didn't—" Jed groaned.

Langthorne copied Elgin's action. "For my fiancée." He slashed Jed's belly in the other direction.

Jed gasped at the sharp new waves of pain. Blood rivulets flowed over his skin from the knife wounds, though he couldn't see them for the box. What was it there for?

Elgin swam into view again. He held a wriggling, squeaking canvas bag at arm's length. Jed's eyes bulged. *Rats!* His muscles spasmed. Elgin pulled the tie-cord undone. He upended the bag and fed its neck through the box's open top.

An avalanche of small, furry bodies pelted Jed's belly. Whiskers tickled him. Tiny paws scrabbled inside the box, piercing his skin with needle claws. His broken wrist-bones grated as he flattened himself against the floor. But the box and the rats moved with him. His fingernails gouged his clenched fists.

Elgin shook the bag until it was empty. He slammed the flap and bolted it shut. Bennet held a huge lump of red-hot coal in his blacksmith's tongs. He placed it on the flap and held it there. A murmur of anticipation ran round the watching crows.

"No," Jed screamed as the metal box heated up and the squeaks changed to squeals and hisses. Uncontrollable tremors shook him. "Please!"

Desperate to evade the heat, the rats attacked the only soft, pliable surface available to them—Jed's belly. They ripped and tore his flesh with savage teeth and claws. He thrashed. He yelled.

The squire handed Bennet a small bag. It chinked as the blacksmith tucked it inside his shirt and left the crypt.

Hour after hour, the rats cut and slashed and gnawed their escape route through Jed's body until his guts burned with fever and the crypt stank of his shit. He begged. He whimpered. His breathing rattled. He floated up to the vaulted roof and found the woman swirling in jasmine clouds, waiting for him.

"I scratched him," she says.

He screamed his innocence, but there was no one to listen, no one to save him. The crows had long since gone to their beds by then, abandoning him to madness and the rats. When dawn's pale light filtered through the lancet window, he sank unresisting into the endless abyss.

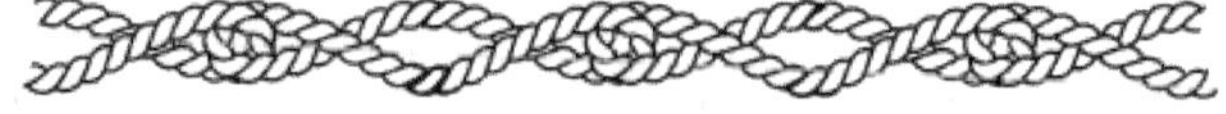

A door thudded. "This way," Megson called. "He's in the crypt." Three sets of footsteps thundered down the staircase and hurried across to Jed's body.

"Sacrilege!" Father Corden cried. "Dear God in Heaven, what inhumanity is this?" He wrenched at one strap buckle whilst the ratcatcher battled with the other until the box came loose and clattered onto the floor. Bloody rats scampered off in all directions.

Megson reached inside Jed's disembowelled belly and fished a snapping rat out by its tail. Father Corden turned aside and spewed his last night's supper up all over the floor. Megson dropped the squirming rat. It ran after the others.

Father Corden wiped his mouth on his sleeve. "The poor wretch is dead," he said. "Tell me you didn't authorize this, Lord Langthorne?"

"He had a fair trial. The evidence against him was incontrovertible." The squire shrugged. "Twelve good men and true, myself included, found him guilty of viciously raping and murdering the unfortunate Miss Elgin." He slid a finger inside his collar to loosen it where the starched fabric chafed the raw scratch on his neck. "Our verdict was unanimous. Jed Suggitt deserved to die for his heinous crimes."

Rosetta Yorke lives in the wilds of North Yorkshire, UK. She writes horror, time travel and Gothic romance short stories. She traces her love of all things dark back to her archaeological days spent 'six feet under' releasing restless skeletons from centuries-old graves in a race against time before the earthen side walls crumbled in on her, or municipal contractors redeveloped the site. Her short stories and drabbles have been published in anthologies by Black Hare Press, HorrorAddicts.net, Dark Rose Press, and Dragon Soul Press. Reach out to her at linktr.ee/rosettayorke

Babylon Burning

Elizabeth Broadbent

Whenever his children or his children's children or the children that came after clamored about the War, Townsend Trenholm remembered the pale, cautious sunshine of that January afternoon in 1865, when he was twelve.

It sidled through the bare, black branches above his cousin's cabin and seemed to bear in itself the scent of wet winter mud. The slaves had fled two days before. His grandmother said the hope of Sherman's invasion had finally ruined them, and when Cypress Bend rose at the thin, strangled crow of their last remaining rooster, they found cabins empty, storehouses looted to empty shelves, and shoals of barefoot prints leading from the quarters to the trackless wastes of Congaree's vast, malarial swampland. Stray chicken feathers and hog prints followed behind. The tattered troop of Negros had stolen everything—*taken what was rightfully theirs*, Town might have said a long time later, but back then his grandmother called them dirty thieves and wept bitter-righteous tears. *Didn't we care for them the best we could,* she said. *This's how they pay us. Lookit that. You can't trust 'em. I always said you can't trust 'em and I was right, I was right all along.*

Two days after that rank treason, after a frantic scuttle to bury the family silver, his cousin Lucas was sent hunting, and Town's grandmother dispatched him to check that those Negros had not perpetrated unspeakable deeds upon their wayward cousin Sylvia and her bastard baby, whose father she steadfastly refused to name. She sent along with him the gardener, their second cousin Randolph, spared soldiering on account on his withered right hand. "A cripple and a boy," Randolph said as they left the lonely barnyard, clean and neat as a tomb because there was nothing to do but keep it that way. "That's the best men Cypress Bend can muster, 'cause all the rest are dead."

Like a schoolhouse rhyme, Town could have recited the Trenholm family losses: his brother Sully, killed at Second Manassas; Uncle Ashby, killed at Fredericksburg; his father Lyons, dead at Cold Harbor. His cousin Henry had not been seen since Gettysburg and they presumed him dead too. *I ain't a boy*, he could have told Randolph. *I'll fight Sherman if he gets close, you see if I don't.*

You're all of twelve years old, Randolph would have said, then he would have cut his iron-colored eyes sideways and added in a voice ugly as a blacksmith's rasp, *Skinny, too.* And Town would have been ashamed, so he kept silent and fingered the Stranger coin in his pocket, kept for luck though luck ran watery-weak. Maybe the slaves would find Strangers in the swamp.

Trenholm cousins whispered about them when their mothers were rolling bandages. *A man came covered in skins, and they said he spoke no language they'd ever heard of, like an Indian but he wasn't an Indian, small and strange in the face,* his cousin Lucas had said, and Town resented the six months between them, how those two slim seasons lent his cousin a wisdom he could never touch. *That was one, he came when our great-grandfather was building our house. And another, in machine-made clothes who spoke perfect English, she came later. She held a bright-shining box in her hand, and she cried all the time, but she said she'd never seen so many stars.*

Beyond splintered fences forlorn with dry-rot and pastures thick and high and brown because there was no stock to graze them, Town and Randolph passed onto the swamp path where wan sun laced through the branch filigree above. No birds sang, and in the winter chill, no mosquitoes bit. They slogged through soughs and guts and muck to Sylvia's cabin of rough-hewn cypress logs, which hunkered atop a clump of earth like an animal readying for winter.

"Quiet," Randolph said, which Town could not parse as command or observation. A poorly woven fence surrounded rabbit-nibbled collards and spinach greens; a wide and silent swamp stream curled off into the distance beyond. Sunshine dappled the half-tamed cabin and its feral little barn. As he stood under that fragile light shining like lacework through the winter branches, Town suddenly and sickeningly recalled Sherman not forty miles off burning Orangeburg. When he finished the general would march on Charleston or Columbia or perhaps Lower Congaree.

"Don't hear that bastard of hers," Randolph said.

"His name's John." Town stepped up to the window and knocked. Sylvia's single room contained unfashionable castoffs from the main house, overlarge in the small space and ill fit to rot in a steam-choked cypress swamp.

Back turned to Town, Sylvia was tucking a man-shape into the high tester bed shoved into a corner.

"I'm coming," she told him.

If Randolph saw the man-shape he would drag it from the bed and beat it; the holy and righteous moral fury of every other female Trenholm would once again descend upon the unbowed dark head of his cousin Sylvia, already exiled to this hermetic swamp-outpost as punishment for her sin. Town scuttled to the door. "She's coming," he said. "She was just making the bed."

Sylvia stepped through the door with her baby in her arms. His eyes were overlarge for his face, but despite the pallor of ill nutrition, he watched them with the bright curiosity of a fox cub. Town reached for him, and Sylvia passed him over.

"What were you doing in there?" Randolph asked.

"I was making the bed, like Town told you," Sylvia said.

"Grandmother sent us to check on you because the slaves ran away two days ago," Town told her. "They took all the food that wasn't stored in the main house. And Sherman is burning Orangeburg prob'ly right now, we had a rider come by yesterday and tell us."

Taking up a pinestraw broom as if she could not waste even a moment with speech, Sylvia swept at the dirt, which did nothing that Town could see but stir up fine, ageless dust. "They raided the gardens?" she asked.

"They took everything," he said.

"I'll send you home with collards," she told him.

He opened his mouth to argue that she was alone with the baby and therefore needed the greens more than they did, since they had at least the canned foods in the pantry, when a wrenching, agonized moan erupted from the house.

"Who the hell was that?" Randolph hefted the wrist-thick, grayish cudgel hauled through two miles of rank swampland. Sylvia simply watched him. It was the same look Town remembered her giving his mother and grandmother when she stood in their airless front parlor, barefoot and bigbellied. Those blackclad women had battered her relentlessly as a stormtide rising on the Ashley River, but Sylvia had shown no expression in those dark eyes, no malice or sadness or sign of regret, but had gone on looking as if she was staring not at women but at some reflection of humanity itself. *She's insolent and slatternly,* Town's mother had said after, and Town had thought that was not quite right.

"I asked you what the hell that was," Randolph said again, which counted as one more insult against her; he did not apologize for his language in front of a lady and a child besides. "Who's in your house, Sylvia?"

But she only went on looking at him in that clearing under the hollow January sun. If Town sniffed hard and deep he imagined he could smell the smoke of a burning city forty miles off. The silver was buried deep. They had nothing else worth stealing but their pride and maybe not even that anymore.

"You got one of them Negros in your house?" Randolph asked. "You tell me now and maybe I'll go easy on them."

Sylvia remained still and silent as those winter trees. The baby in Town's arms did not squirm. Randolph shoved his cudgel into the door and pushed it open.

"No," Sylvia said quietly, and once only.

A string of blistering invective rose as Randolph stomped into the cabin. Town imagined muddy prints marring her clean wood, then heard a sick thump as a man hit the floorboards. "You got a goddamn Yankee in here!" Randolph shouted. "You traitor whore, you got a Yankee soldier in your bed!"

She shouted something like *he's not* and dashed into the house. Town set the baby in that fine-sifted dust. He sat up with his fat hands planted in the earth and his bright eyes the same shade as the high, cold sky. Town loved Sylvia. But he hated Yankees more, and he ran.

Muck sucked his feet, which had long worn out any shoes the world might have to offer, and since his brother's still flopped hopelessly, Town ran unshod through wet-splattering mud clotted thick with last year's leaf-skeletons, his Stranger coin clutched tight in his fist though he was too old to believe in it. *We're finished,* his mother had said. *My son doesn't have any shoes to wear. I never thought I'd descend so far into poverty that my son would have no shoes.* Smilax vine tore at his mended and tattering pants. His brother and father and uncle and cousin had flung themselves into the maul of war so Yankees would never come to Cypress Bend and now they had come anyway. They had bled out on battlefields in Virginia and maybe Pennsylvania and they died in vain, because the Yankees had come to burn them out and take what was theirs. When Town reached the main house he was nearly wheezing with exhaustion and fear he would never admit to, but he hurled himself onto the porch and threw open the door and shouted, "*Yankees!* Sylvia has a Yankee soldier in her house!"

In a farther room, high pure terror-screams erupted from his sisters and cousins. A moment later his mother and his aunts Eleanor and Nelia and Caroline fluttered in, still clutching homespun bandages, his grandmother behind. Rail-thin and blackclad, they moved in tandem, like a flock of crows. "Repeat yourself without hysteria, Townsend Trenholm," his grandmother said.

"We went to check on Sylvia and she had a Yankee soldier in her bed," Town told her.

The old woman had held that plantation together for four long years and her expression said that she would hold it through Judgment Day against God Himself if necessary. "Just one?" she asked.

"Yes," Town told her.

"The Home Guard is too busy to deal with him," his grandmother said. "We'll have to take care of this ourselves."

"Mother, we don't have enough to keep a prisoner fed," Aunt Caroline told her.

His grandmother turned her head with the slow deliberation of a hunting owl. Town would remember that look forever, her eyes narrowing into something flinted and iron hard that he had never seen. This was a woman who not a day before had told them to hide the silver under the manure pile because the Yankees would be too squeamish to dig it up, and when Aunt Eleanor protested, his grandmother told them to pick up shovels or forget about dinner. She had cried about the slaves but ever since something inside her had broken or perhaps come together in a kind of vicious strength Town had never imagined, and it frightened him. "We won't be feeding a prisoner," his grandmother told his aunt. "His people killed Ashby and Lyons and Sullivan. Henry wasn't but a boy."

Aunt Eleanor covered her face with her hands. They generally pretended there was still some hope for Henry. The other women straightened; his grandmother had invoked the holy martyrs.

"Keep rolling bandages," she said. "Randolph will bring him along. Thank you for telling us, Townsend. There's plenty of firewood stacked around the cabin, and Lucas came back not half an hour ago. You two pile it all near the Meeting Oak."

"Yessum," he said. Town knew better than to ask questions. Since his grandmother had stopped crying, she granted no quarter and brooked no opposition; he would do it, and he would not ask why. Lucas was mending a belt on the back veranda, his hound dog at his feet. He fed it on fox squirrel but it stayed bone-thin and hungry-mean. "Why d'you think we're piling wood?" he asked as they walked back to the cabins.

"I think she wants to get us away from the house," Town said. Then, because for once there were no women or sisters or little brothers around, he asked, "Do you think the Negros will find any Strangers in the swamp?"

"Maybe," Lucas said. "I wish I could see a Stranger. I'd ask them what it was like where they came from."

"Where d'you think they come from?" Town asked.

Lucas held hands out like he was praying or trying to pick up the empty air. "Sully said they're people from Cypress Bend but another time. Like the coins we find. They walk in from that other time and that's what they go back to. He thought the Strangers were Trenholms too, all of 'em, but I think that part's wrong."

Town wished he had never asked, and he hated his cousin suddenly; his brother had told Lucas something he would never say to Town himself, and Sully was dead for a cause that had done no good in the end: the Yankees had come anyway. Henry had sent a letter saying that at Second Manassas, General Gregg backed the men up a hill and unsheathed his old Revolutionary War saber. He cut some daisies and said, "Let us die here, my men, let us die," and Sully did.

They cleaned out the cabins down to the kindling boxes, and it kept them busy until sunset fell in tatters of pink and orange. The cousins were cold-toed and chill-fingered when they finished, and when they came back to the house Randolph was leading their last ribby mule up to the bare-sticked front garden, a limp man slung over its back like a sack. His pants and shirt were dirt-crusted and swamp-stained but unmistakably blue. Sylvia walked behind, the baby in her arms.

"He's not a soldier," she said when she saw Town.

"Sure as hell he is," Randolph said. "You see that blue? She wants to save him."

"I can prove it," she told him. "He has things in the woods. He buried them to keep them safe but when he's not delirious he can say where they are and show them to you. He showed them to me once. I have more in—"

"He's a Yankee," Randolph said. "He talks funny."

"He's not," Sylvia told them. "He—"

Randolph turned and spit. It landed on her bare toes, an indictment that said everything about who she was and what she did against family and country and maybe even God Himself. "Shut up."

Town had a terrible idea, and he opened his mouth to say it but his grandmother came out on the porch then with his mother and aunt, that old crow-flock alighting like a murder landing on a grave. The girls clustered behind them and the little boys peeped through their legs. "You brought him," his grandmother said. "Stand him up."

"He can't stand up," Sylvia said. "He's had ague for two days now."

Town's grandmother stepped from the rest of the women. She had lost his grandfather just after Fort Sumter and her sons Ashby and Lyons to the great Southern Cause that no longer seemed so great or so grand at all after four years of scrambling and starving and now hiding the silver under the manure pile. She had lost her grandson Sully and probably Henry, who went to war instead of college, and Town and Lucas had no shoes. The girls had no fabric for dresses and the women no dye for mourning clothes; the slaves had stolen the last of their pork, which they had no salt to preserve anyway. As the old woman stepped forward, Town saw these outrages carved on her as if they had twisted into her flesh and made his grandmother more than herself, goddess-like in rage and pain and vengeance. He clutched the Stranger coin tight.

"How long has he been at your house?" his grandmother asked, and in that long gray silence that came just before winter twilight, her voice was too quiet.

"Four days," Sylvia said. "I found him half-naked and starved in the swamp when I went out to look for wild ginger. He's not a soldier."

"Then why's he wearing that blue?" Grandmother demanded more than asked, and her tone brooked no disagreement, as if what she said was self-evident and could not be denied.

"He's from somewhere else," Sylvia said.

The man reared upright. Wild-eyed as a frightened horse, his buttoned shirt hung in strips, and he stared around him, gaping and confused. "Been here before but it's different," he said. "On a field trip. I had to write a report."

"He's a Yankee spy!" Lucas shouted. "He said it!"

"No!" Sylvia clutched the baby to her chest. But his grandmother was pointing toward the cabins. She was saying something to Randolph that Town could not make out over his cousin's pleas. The girls were in an uproar of terror that a spy should come to Cypress Bend, because one spy would beget more. His mother and aunts nodded, that crow-flock in solemn agreement with their leader, and then they were all marching down the muddy road toward the cabins with the man clinging to the mule and Sylvia crying and weeping behind. The baby made no sound. Town knew better than to comfort her. Whatever monstrous energy had possessed his grandmother would only come down upon his own head if he dared to speak on her behalf. The man had said—but what if—two impulses warred in him and he did not know which was correct. He knew only that he was twelve years old and blue twilight was falling fast as the night-cold crept in and tightened, tightened. He could not stand against four years of war and death and poverty and silver buried under the manure pile.

"Randolph, drive a sturdy pole next to that woodpile, man-height," his grandmother said when they came near the Meeting Oak. "Hold that mule, Town."

Town had a terrible sick sense about something about to happen, trembling on the cusp of a deed too terrible to contemplate, and though he was frightened of his grandmother he could not make himself obey. Sylvia thrust the baby at him; he grabbed for the child before it fell. Lucas took the mule. Implacable as a god, Randolph drove a stake as the man babbled feverishly about a field trip and a report and a plantation visit. His skin shone pale in the blue-black dark and his eyes showed too much of their whites.

"The Home Guard is busy," his grandmother said. "We're going to take care of this ourselves. I won't waste bullets on a Yankee. We'll burn him like they burn our cities."

"He's not from here!" Sylvia shouted. "I'm telling you, he's a Stranger!"

Her bastard baby might have been a sinful abomination, but Sylvia's words had shattered the last and worst taboo of the Trenholm family. The aunts gaped at her like fish newly hooked and gasping for air; the little ones dropped into confused buzzing. Randolph stared. Cousin Lucas went stiff and silent, as if a woman had uttered words unspeakable and possibly dangerous. Grandmother would step forward and slap her, and Sylvia's head would wrench sideways with the blow—

"You're a liar and we don't believe whores in this house," his grandmother said, that low voice overtaking everything in the grimed twilight, like Town imagined God would sound, His vengeance and His anger. Yankees had taken Sully and Ashby and father and likely Henry, so they would take this man as recompense for the sins of a whole Babylon. This sick man had killed no Trenholm but Town's grandmother would not be swayed. Town knew better than to try. He clenched his Stranger coin tight. *I will not cry I will not cry I will not cry*, he told himself, because he was twelve years old and he would shame himself, even if Randolph was dragging the man from the mule. The gardener yanked the man by his wrists, and his head and heels slammed the unvictorious dirt. His face raked through the firewood, spilling it everywhere, as Randolph shunted him upright and lashed him to the stake.

"Town! Lucas! Pile that wood up right!" His grandmother pointed imperiously as one of the Furies themselves. From sheer habit of obedience, Town gave Sylvia the baby. All panic gone, she wore that dark-eyed look he remembered from the parlor. "Leave now," she told him then. "Or you'll remember this for the rest of your life, and you've seen enough already."

Randolph was tying the man's chest to the stake. He moaned low and desperate, a deep-sea creature heaved on a beach. Town and Lucas scrabbled at his feet like beetles and heaped up the wood that would become his hell and his doom.

—Then they will weep and wail at the sight of the fire that consumes her, Babylon—Woe, woe to the great city, your hour has come

Town could not break away from that fragment, as if in this strange extremity his mind insisted on clinging stubbornly to the known and familiar. His grandmother held a box of Lucifer matches, and as she strode down the porch steps she seemed in the gathering dark to be too tall and too broad to be a woman; she had become an embodiment of pure Southern vengeance. The man's eyes had closed. He slumped, as if in his sickness he had given himself over to her. Vestal, beautiful in a vengeance indiscreet, she knelt and struck the match.

Town ran.

His feet slapped the mud and for the second time that day, he ran down that swamp path. He held the Stranger coin tight, tight, almost certain then and terrified in his certainty, ignoring the smilax vine lashing his pants and the black swamp pressing on every side, unknowable and unsettled. Behind him, screams rose like the smoke of a burning city. The man had caught fire. In the midst of that sickness, his fever had become flames, that conflagration born of war and poverty, privation and defeat. Town understood as he bolted through that forest that his grandmother had burnt—was burning, the man was screaming and he was burning—that man as one final act of revenge against a world that stole away her sons and her slaves and her plantation and the very social order she believed in blood and bone and body and soul.

Those thin high screams of undeath trailed Town until he was no longer certain if he heard them or supplied them in his own grim fearful certainty. He ran until his breath jerked in his lungs and wheezed in his throat, until his palms slammed the rough wood door of his cousin's cabin and he shoved inside. The coals were still burning, and on the table next to the bed he found what he was looking for, what he dreaded: three coins. *United States of America,* they read. *In God We Trust.* And the dates: *1981, 1983, 1986.* Next to it, he found a strange watch, one with numbers instead of hands, without a winding mechanism. 6:47 changed to 6:48, a miraculous shift that could only happen through what Town might call magic.

Holding his Stranger coin tight, Town dropped to the floor next to that cast-off bed in the small swamp-cabin, trying not to cry for all he'd lost. Though he was twelve years old and ought to know better, he failed. *I will never go back*, he decided. *I will never go back to them and their madness and their Confederate dead and their manure pile silver.*

John had no father. Sylvia had no husband. Now, Town would have no family. Shuddering, in a glorious fever of grief and relief and hope, he hunkered down to wait for her.

Elizabeth Broadbent (she/her) left the South Carolina swamps for the Commonwealth of Virginia, where she fights bisexual erasure while living with her three sons and husband. She's the author of *Naked & Famous*, *Ink Vine* (Undertaker Books), and *Blood Cypress*, coming in 2025 with Raw Dog Screaming Press. Her speculative fiction has appeared with *HyphenPunk*, *Tales to Terrify*, *If There's Anyone Left*, *Peunumbric*, and *The Cafe Irreal*, among others. During her long career as a journalist, her nonfiction appeared in places such as *The Washington Post*, *Insider*, and *ADDitude Magazine*.

On Horseback They Carried Thunder

Scotty Milder

The posse found the two b'hoys at dusk.

The older one—Chick Denton—tried to dry gulch the three men. That was a mistake. Everyone knew Brady was one of the Rangers what cut down Sam Bass and his gang of high binders north of Austin a few years back. Brady'd been in a dozen shootouts since, and had never been so much as winged.

So what Chick done was pure beshitted panic. He heard hooves charging down the Poison Mesa—Brady's quarter horse, followed by Carlos's brokedown old mare and Estancia's bangtail mustang—and he came out from behind some scrub oak, hollering like a crackbrain caught in a conniption fit. That was bad enough, but it probably wouldn't have gotten him beefed by itself.

No. What got him done for was the Colt.

Carlos didn't have a chance to reach for the Stoeger before that Colt went *ka-BLAM*. Carlos's mare reared back, whinnying. Carlos grabbed the apple and held on for dear life before he got grassed. Something whizzed past his ear and *thwocked* into a pine behind him.

There was another big boom off to his right, and—just like some bill-show magic trick—the top of Chick's head came off in a spray of blood and brains. The expression on Chick's face never changed—not even when he crumpled, face first, to the pine needles.

"A'ight!" Brady barked. In his confusion, Carlos thought he was yelling at Chick's corpse. The LeMat revolver was in Brady's hand; Carlos never saw him draw, but now he saw the smoke trickling from the barrel. The reek of gunpowder hung thick and mixed uneasily with the mountain bouquet of distant wood smoke and pine sap. "You best come out them bushes, Linc, 'fore I have to come in after you!"

Presently there came a sob, and then the second b'hoy—the younger one, old Thomas Cartwright's chap, Linc—popped up from the leaves. He looked pale as milk, the freckles standing out like the French Pox. His red hair was damp with sweat.

"I ain't armed!" he yelled in a high, quavering voice. He thrust his hands over his head. "I ain't got no gun or nothin'!"

"Yeah, well, you keep on grabbin' at the sky." Brady swung out of his saddle. He holstered the LeMat, then reached into his saddle bag and pulled out a coil of catgut rope.

Linc Cartwright's eyes bulged.

"Whatcha doin' with that?" he cried. His arms began to drop.

It finally occurred to Carlos to do his job; he looped the Stoeger around, dropped it into his hands, and raised it. Linc saw the shotgun swing toward him, and his hands shot back into the air.

"Don't you worry none," Brady said as he uncoiled the rope. "You just keep on grabbin'."

Carlos glanced over at Estancia, who remained hunched over his saddle horn, watching without much interest. Estancia caught his look. His single eye glimmered with cruel amusement. The burned-out, fleshy cavern of the missing other caught the dying sunlight and, to Carlos, seemed to fill with blood.

Estancia sneered, showing stubs of brown teeth. He loosed a stream of chaw into the pine needles as Brady clomped toward the blubbering boy.

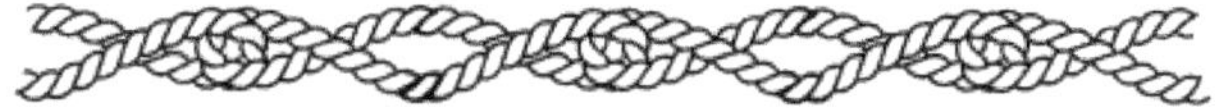

It was two nights ago that someone busted into the two-room cabin behind Boone Bailey's livery, where Boone's wife Greta and their nineteen-year-old daughter Eleanor lay sleeping.

Eleanor just happened to be there. She'd been hitched up the year before to a bug eater from Nebraska named Bart Jewitt. Bart had come west into New Mexico to work the Beaubian-Miranda Grant in Colfax County. Most everyone agreed that he was dumb as an ox and three times as ugly, but he was steady and God fearing and seemed kind enough—as bug eaters went—and the general belief was that Eleanor had done well for herself. Bart was on a cattle drive, so she'd ridden down to stay with her folks until he made his way back.

Boone was over to Tollerson's, which was as lowdown a doggery as could be found in any of the cow towns dotting the plains of San Miguel County. Boone Bailey was a steady hand with the horses, but he was a mean old wolfer who was too partial to Hugh Tollerson's coffin varnish. He didn't misuse Greta with his hands, so far as anyone knew, but folks were known to whisper that it may not be the most un-Christian notion to suppose Greta might be better off if Boone somehow found his way into the bone orchard sooner rather than later.

So that's how it came to be that Greta and Eleanor were home alone when whoever it was came calling. No one heard what transpired, which for months afterward was the source of much chatter. The livery was right in the middle of town, after all, and what was done to Greta and Eleanor was...well, it was hard to imagine any of it happened quietly.

Both women were beaten raw, after rags were stuffed into their mouths to muffle the crying. The mother was tied up and made to watch as whoever it was had their way with the daughter. Then both women's throats were cut.

When Boone came stumbling in, the blood was just starting to harden into the oiled dirt floor. Boone careened off down the street, waking folks all through town as he bellowed for the sheriff.

George Brady and Carlos Quintana came answering.

In truth, Brady wasn't no sheriff. The actual sheriff was over in Las Vegas, which was half a day's ride to the west, where the New Mexico plains began their rise into the jagged teeth of the Sangre de Cristos. But everyone had heard about how maybe it was Brady's bullet that took down Sam Bass in Round Rock, so no one objected when he took up the marshal's star. People took to calling him "Sheriff" because it seemed right and proper to do so.

Carlos was twenty-two and green as a summer sapling when he went to Brady for the deputy's job.

"I ain't never worked with a Mexican before," Brady'd said. "Not sure I'm fixin' to start now."

"All due respect, sir, I ain't no Mexican," Carlos responded. "My people been 'round here for two hundred years."

Brady lifted a bushy white eyebrow. "You lookin' to sass me, boy?"

Carlos restrained an impulse to call the uppish old gringo "señor."

"No, sir."

"All right, then."

Carlos had the job.

That was just over a year ago. All in all, they got on well enough. Up to that night at Boone Bailey's cabin, there really hadn't been a lot to the job, anyway. But the moment Carlos came in and nearly choked on the blood stench—and then looked at Eleanor Jewitt and saw the red mouth that had been carved across her throat—he knew it had all changed. Whatever lies he'd allowed himself to believe about being a lawman before, he was about to learn the raw, bloody truth of it now.

He'd glanced over at Brady, who was gazing dispassionately at what was left of the mother. She'd been kicked into the far corner like a pile of discarded clothes.

Brady looked up at him. The hardness in those gray eyes made Carlos back up a step.

"A'ight," Brady said. "Let's get going."

Brady looped the catgut around Linc Cartwright's neck and threw the other end over to Carlos.

"Toss it over that branch yonder," he said.

"T'wan't me!" Linc blubbered. His gaze was fixed on Brady. "I didn't have nothin' to do with what happened to them ladies!"

"Then why'd you run?" Carlos asked. He was genuinely curious.

Linc's wet eyes rolled to him. Carlos saw hope in those quivering jellies, and wished he'd kept his trap shut.

"'Cause we knew y'all was after us!" he brayed. "Word got back to Chick's pa that the old preacher from that blueskin church up the way told y'all he saw us comin' out'n livery with them horses, and we was afeared so we run. I *knows* it was stupid. I *knows* it now. But—"

"Tell you what *I* know," Brady said. "I know that feller there—" he gestured toward Chick, who had mostly stopped leaking his juices into the dirt, "—was sweet on Eleanor, back when she was still an angelica."

"I—"

"—*And* I know that after she'd passed him over for Bart, Chick was known to get good and boozily down to Tollerson's, and then start in with all his blusterations to whichever bronc buster, bar dog, or calico queen would hear him blather about how he was gonna take that apple peeler of his and open old Bart from groin to sternum. All for stealin' a girl what wanted nothin' to do with him in the first place. That about the heft of it?"

"I—"

"No need to flap that bazoo, I already got the truth," Brady said. "So mayhap you chuckleheads went over there, all blue on Tollerson's dynamite, and mayhap that dynamite got Chick to thinkin' on doin' exactly what he been talkin' about. Or mayhap—and this here is what *I* think, 'though it don't matter to naught now but the Lord God above—Chick heard Eleanor was in town, and y'all went there full split, two lowdown yella-bellies because y'all knew Bart was gone on the drive, and a pair of cryin' ladies go down easier than a bug eater who's handy with a barking iron, ain't that so? How's it all sound to you, Carlos? Sound like a tale as old as time?"

It did. And something about that bothered Carlos immensely. It was the perfect story, and fit all the facts as comfortable as a wool mitten. Maybe *too* comfortable.

Estancia grunted.

"I'm done talkin'," Brady said. "Carlos, climb on down off that horse. Let's get this done."

Brady delivered a swift kick to the back of Linc's knees. Linc went down with a squawk. At the very same instant, Brady yanked hard on the catgut, cutting the b'hoy's squeal off.

Carlos swung out of his saddle and glanced over at Estancia. Estancia cradled a Winchester lever-action, vaguely aiming the rifle at Linc like Brady had commanded. Carlos wouldn't copper a bet as to what Estancia would do if the kid tried to run or fight back, though. Estancia was a trapper from the hills outside Mora. Carlos's family had been in New Mexico for two hundred years; Estancia's had probably been there for half again the number. If he spoke a word of English, he hadn't yet deigned to, at least not in their company. He'd taken

Brady's money without objection—and agreed to help track the fugitives north as they blundered their clumsy trail into the mountains past Taos toward the no-man's land around Poison Mesa—but Carlos hadn't missed the contemptuous boil in the old Hispano's remaining eye as he sized up the gringo lawman and his young deputy. The contempt hovered around Estancia like corpse-stink, even if Brady himself was too arrogant to smell it.

Carlos suspected that Estancia was one of the Brotherhood. Even to Carlos, whose own roots went back to the days of the land grants, the Brotherhood was so mysterious as to be the stuff of legend. He'd grown up with whispered tales about the secret society of flagellants that hid in the Sangre de Cristos, scourging themselves with thorns and re-enacting the crucifixion with actual hammers and nails. The Brotherhood had been born of necessity after the Mexican War of Independence left the Northern Territories to fend for themselves. The Brotherhood looked after their own.

Everyone knew that—if you wanted to keep your blood flowing inside your body—you did not cross the Brotherhood.

"Carlos!" Brady shouted, annoyed.

Carlos wrenched his eyes back to the old man. "Yessir," he said, and tossed the rope over the branch. It creaked, but held.

"Ain't I supposed to get no trial?" Linc brayed.

"No need to waste time down at the Las Vegas hoosegow," Brady drawled. "Old Judge Milsap's a skeersome Baptist type from Oklahoma, and his brother's the local sinbuster. They're not like to go any easier on you."

He wrenched Linc's hands behind his back and bound them with an old bandana.

"We was just takin' the horses so's we could sell 'em!" Lincoln screamed. "We was in the livery and we heard the ladies kickin' up a devilish fuss. We got afeared so cut and we run. And then when Chick's pa—"

"Christ on a hobblin' crutch, son, you could talk a donkey's hind leg off," Brady said.

Estancia muttered under his breath. Carlos threw him a look. Estancia caught it and quickly shook his head.

"You got any prayers you want to say before you swing?" Brady asked.

"*Please!*" Linc's eyes went to Carlos.

"You're wastin' time to get right with God, son," Brady said. "I'm gonna count down from ten, and then Carlos there's gonna yank on that rope and you're gonna dangle. If you don't say your prayers now, it'll be old Sam Hill waitin' for you, ready to stick his fork up your ass, not Saint Peter with the keys to the Kingdom."

Linc held Carlos's gaze.

"You knows I didn't do it, Carlos! I knows you know it!"

"Ten," Brady said. "Nine...eight—"

"Carlos—!"

"Seven—"

"Come on—!"

"Six—"

"Ah fuck—"

"Five—"

"OhLordJesuscleansemefrom—

"Four—"

"—myunrighteousnessforgiveme—"

"Three—"

"—ofallmysinsmove—"

"Two—"

"—intomyheartImakeyoumyLordand—"

"One. Do it, Carlos."

"—Saviorthankyoufor—"

"*Do it!*"

Carlos's hand tightened on the rope. But he didn't pull.

"—yoursacrificeIaccept—"

The sun hovered just over the flat roof of Poison Mesa, casting bands of red fire into the vermillion sky.

Brady's eyes blazed over the top of Linc's head. His big flat teeth jutted from behind his white mustache like tombstones.

"Do it, you bean eater, 'fore I come over there and give you a lacing!"

"—yourgiftofeternalsalvationamen!" Linc finished.

Carlos pulled the rope.

Linc Cartwright wasn't big, but he was heavy enough and Carlos was no muscled bulldozer himself. His arms and his back strained with the effort—especially once Linc's feet started pinwheeling as if he were caught in a runoff stream and kicking against the current.

Finally, Brady ambled over and picked up the catgut that lay coiled at Carlos' feet. He wrapped it around his forearm and added his weight to the pull. The branch creaked again. Linc rose another foot off the ground. His throat made gruesome, inhuman noises. It didn't sound like what Carlos figured a person choking to death would sound like. Carlos had read *Moby-Dick* and *Twenty Thousand Leagues Under the Sea* and any number of penny dreadfuls that cribbed from those better books, and even though he had no hopes of ever seeing the ocean himself, what the air in Linc's neck was doing sounded to him like what he imagined one of those strange undersea creatures would sound like if it somehow flopped out of those watery depths and found itself drying out on some distant beach somewhere.

You don't need to watch, Carlos thought. *You can't help but listen to him die, but there ain't nothin' sayin' you can't find somethin' else to look at.*

From somewhere far off, Carlos heard another sound: high and rhythmic, softly metallic. It was almost like the distant bong of church bells, or the ding of a longcase clock striking midnight, or the tinkle of wind chimes in a light breeze. Or maybe it was something going wrong inside his own head, his heart—something rebelling at what he was seeing, what he was *doing.* He didn't know.

Look away, he told himself again.

The dire sounds coming out of Linc began to taper off. His kicking slackened to feeble jerks.

Damn you, just look away!

But he kept watching. In the end, he watched the entire thing.

That ringing, whatever it was, never stopped. Not until it was over.

Brady smoked a foul-smelling quirley as Carlos wrapped both corpses in tan canvas sheets and bound them by lantern light.

Estancia simply sat on a rock and sucked on a mouthful of chaw. He watched Carlos work with careful interest, but didn't offer any sort of help.

Carlos would have thought Chick would've been the worst—what with all the gruel spilling out of the crater in the top of his head—but somehow it was Linc that got to him. The b'hoy was still warm, for one thing, and the pliant way his limbs flopped all about as Carlos tried to maneuver him onto the canvas made his stomach flop all around like a shot dog. And there was the fact that, when Carlos rolled him over, his eyes were still buggy. The whites were as pink as a summer sunset.

Looking into them, Carlos realized he knew two things with utter certainty:

The first was that Linc was telling the truth when he said he and Chick Denton didn't beef the Bailey women.

The second was that George Brady knew it.

Carlos didn't know what to do with this knowledge. Not out here, in the dark under the looming shadow of Poison

Mesa—which was now a hulking black immensity against the shimmering carpet of stars, a thing that felt alive and watchful and somehow tallowy with menace—with just himself and Brady and this strange Hispano tracker who, so far as Carlos knew, didn't speak a word of English. Carlos knew a few words of Spanish, enough to serve as a half-ass translator for Brady's commands. But he'd been raised out in the eastern plains amongst the gringos, and had long ago taken on the gringo's language and ways. And right now, the gringo's way was to keep his damn trap shut and get his damn self home without any extra holes in his damn body.

By the time he was done with the bodies, Brady was gazing thoughtfully past the trees. The yellow lantern light made him look ancient and ghastly, as if he'd somehow shriveled to a husk while Carlos worked.

"It's late," he said. "We oughta bed down for the night."

Estancia made a noise. Carlos looked over at the tracker and saw him frowning.

So he does understand, Carlos thought. *Interesting.*

"*Qué pasa?*" Carlos asked.

Estancia loosed a stream of chaw and rattled off something. The words were mushy, and Carlos missed most of them. But he got the gist.

"What's he on the prod about?" Brady asked.

"Somethin' about the mesa," Carlos said. "And I think he said 'white man.' Means you, I reckon."

"S'pose he must," Brady agreed, and went to his quarter horse. He started unstrapping his flea-trap. "Tell him he's free to ride off, if he's feelin' pokerish. But if'n he wants the rest of his money, he'll stick around and make sure we make it least as far as the E-town turnoff on the 'morrow."

Estancia grunted and flapped a hand.

"I think he gets it," Carlos said.

"I reckon so," Brady said, dropping his flea-trap to the dirt. "I reckon he does at that."

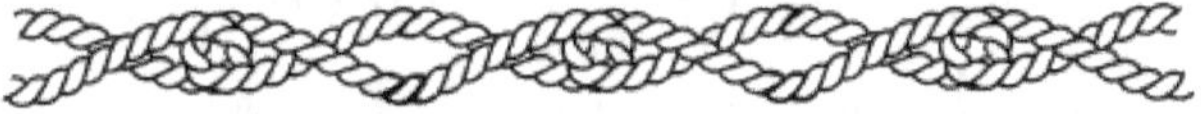

Carlos woke to the ghostly near-harmony of distant chimes and—much closer—a wet, tearing sound.

A dream stuck its claws into him. He didn't understand it, but even as sleep drained away and he ascended into wakefulness, its images refused to let loose their grip.

He saw a man's face, indistinct and with a ghostly pallor, bobbing through some sort of miasmic green-gray haze. He couldn't quite get a handle on the features; the face was plain to the point of impalpability, and later—as he rode the many miles home in silence—he'd reflect back upon the nightmare, trying to excavate its memory, mine it for further definition. He would do this for many years after, on occasion finding himself laying ill at ease upon his bed, first alone and eventually beside his wife, sometimes listening to the snap and yodel of coyotes out in the grassy plains, sometimes the drone of crickets or the howl of wind, sometimes just his wife's untroubled snoring, or maybe—on those nights where the younglings were restless and she bunked down with them in their beds—simply the empty press of nothing at all.

Those empty nights were the worst, because it was in those void-like hours where he most often found himself quarrying his recollections, conjuring up that ashen face, trying and always failing to delineate it, to situate its physiognomy within some determinable boundary, a firm and perceptible outline, that his wakeful mind could comprehend, and the more that boundary crumbled, that outline softened, the specific characteristics of that face skittered out of reach, the more he'd begin to imagine that out in the untenanted plains beyond his window he could hear the metallic clink of chimes.

It's just that you're afeared, Padre Ortega would tell him one Sunday in the confessional booth, when Carlos would try to explain it. *You're afeared, and that fear creates a hole, and your mind goes and fills it for you.*

Is it my mind what's filling it? Carlos would ask him. *Can't it be the Devil, workin' his way with me?*

The Padre didn't have an answer.

So there was that face, pale as moonlight in a sooty haze. There was also the low, red-orange glow of a coal fire and, atop it, something like a jawbone studded with teeth. They weren't human teeth, but rather a jagged row of shimmering white knobs like saw teeth. There was the Poison Mesa itself, its flat summit cloaked in darkness except for a strange, greenish-white glow that wafted like smoke down its craggy slope.

And then he was awake.

There was no more fire. It had burned down to cracklings, and the chill sliced through Carlos's thin blanket like knives. He shivered the last remnants of sleep away and sat up.

The distant plink and tinkle of chimes remained. They drifted down from behind him. From the mesa.

A shadow crouched on the other side of the dead fire, its rounded shoulders heaving as it worked. There was that tearing sound. Something squelched in the dark.

And then: a hard, stony scrape. Carlos immediately recognized that as the sound of a blade being dragged across bone.

The Stoeger lay beside him. Slowly, he reached for it.

The shadow stopped. The scraping ceased. Now he heard only the chimes, along with someone's ragged breathing and the steady *drip...drip...drip...* of liquid pattering to dirt.

A low voice came out of the darkness:

"You don't need that, *hermano*."

The voice was filled with gravel, dense with the accent of the Sangre de Cristos.

Estancia.

"What are you doing?"

Carlos heard the scratch of sulfur against a fingernail. Match light flared, and then the warm glow of the lantern suffused the camp.

Estancia raised the lantern. Carlos had a moment to see that the old Hispano was painted in blood before Estancia lowered the lantern and showed him his work.

"Oh..." Carlos moaned, and clapped a horrified hand to his mouth.

Estancia lifted Brady's head—which was separated from his body—and looked at it without much interest. One of Brady's eyes drooped slightly, showing a sliver of white in the amber glow. The other was swollen shut. His lower teeth glistened through the chalky, gore-spattered bristles of his mustache.

Estancia tossed the head away, beyond the reach of the lantern's light. Carlos listened to the thump and crack of it tumbling through the brush and felt his stomach lurch.

Estancia wiped his knife on his pant leg and sheathed it.

"You'll want to wrap this one like the others," he said, nodding toward Brady's headless body. Carlos now found he couldn't tear his eyes away from the ragged stump of neck. "Take it back to his wife. I'm sure she'll want to give him a Christian burial. Not that he deserves it."

His English is perfect, Carlos thought madly. *He understood every damn word that we said.*

"Why? Why would you—?"

Estancia sneered. His one eye caught the lantern glow and blazed with holy light. A bit of the Bible rocketed through Carlos's head: *Thy sons have fainted, they lie at the head of all the streets, as a wild bull in a net...they are full of the fury of the LORD, the rebuke of thy God.*

"Don't ask me *that, hermano.*"

Carlos looked down at what was left of Brady—the old gringo lawman who supposedly took down Sam Bass, and did ever Carlos *really* believe that? Did he truly cotton to those big stories of righteous gunfights and curly wolf outlaws brought virtuously to heel? After a year of working under the man, getting to know him and his bunk, would Carlos pay a single Boston dollar for even one of those tales. Or did he in his heart believe they were all so much bosh and Barnum?

And didn't he notice how Brady used to linger over Eleanor Bailey in those days before she became Eleanor Jewitt? She was a pretty thing, fresh as clean laundry hanging on the line, and didn't Carlos see how Brady leered at her on the boardwalk in front of Greenberg's dry goods or Montoya's barbershop? Brady always hid it under a veneer of gentlemanly graces, but Carlos wasn't anyone's fool, and he knew what that lizardy glint really meant. He knew what kind of thoughts danced around in the sour meat of the old man's skull.

He just never would've imagined a man such as he could ever act upon them.

"Don't ask me that, hermano. You know why."

Carlos nodded. "I...I suppose I do."

Estancia gazed into the darkness beyond Carlos, to where the chimes continued to echo down Poison Mesa's slopes.

"I know you hear them, too," he said. "He waits."

"What? *Who?*"

"El hombre pálido," Estancia said. *"Look."*

Carlos turned.

The mesa was a long, pitch-black shadow hulking into the darkened sky. It rose from the valley floor in strange angles that seemed nearly impossible in the flatness of the night. Its top was table smooth, save for two jutting formations on the southwestern edge; one was columnar and oddly curved, like a bent finger. The other bulged from the mesa's side like a tumor.

Something glowed between those formations. The light was faint, almost imperceptible, but the longer Carlos stared the less he could deny it was there. It was cool and vaguely phantasmic, its greenish hue unlike anything he'd seen before.

At least not during his waking hours.

"He waits for you," Estancia said.

"Why me?" Carlos breathed.

"You were a part of it," Estancia said. "So was I, *en verdad, pero* I did not pull the rope, so maybe he will leave me alone? Only time will tell, but I'm an old man and I'm part of the Brotherhood, so I don't worry overmuch about these things. I pray to Jesus for forgiveness, and I ask the Virgin Mother for her blessings, and I hope that maybe when I die I will be judged a good man. But I leave all that to the Father's judgment. It is not for me to decide. But you pulled the rope. *You* did that, not me. So he waits for you, *en la mesa, en la luz verde.* He would have come and taken you already, but I did what I could. I left a token for him to take back into his darkness."

"The head," Carlos said. Acid washed up from his stomach and burned his throat.

Estancia nodded.

"All we can do is hope it is enough."

"Is...it the devil?" Carlos asked.

Estancia didn't answer for a long time. They listened to the chimes, and the creaking of pine branches in the wind. They watched the glow. It seemed to pulse between the formations, like a heartbeat.

Finally:

"Nobody knows what he is. He's just *el hombre pálido*, and he's always been here. But he's why we never come this far. The Indians stay away. The Brotherhood stays away. I shouldn't have let us sleep here but..."

He looked down at Brady's corpse.

"*Estaba curioso.*"

Carlos's mouth was dry. He licked his lips, and it was like his tongue was made of thorns.

"You should wrap him. I'll help you tie them all to the old man's horse." Estancia stood. He threw one last glance toward the mesa. At that uncanny light.

"Then we should leave."

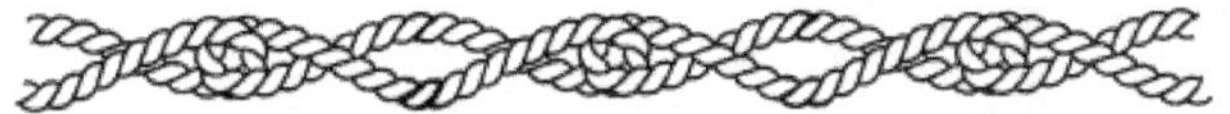

Before they parted a day later in the tree-studded foothills of Capulin Peak, where the trail forked south toward Mora and east toward Elizabethtown, Carlos asked Estancia what he should tell them when he showed up with two dead b'hoys and Brady's headless body.

"Blame it on me, *hermano*," Estancia said, and laughed his gravel-filled laugh. "If they want to come after me, let them. Just be sure to let them know they'll be coming after the Brotherhood."

Carlos nodded. "That'll sure make them think twice."

Estancia loosed a stream of brown chaw and regarded Carlos with his one eye.

"He's got his mark on you, *hermano*," Estancia said. "Don't you ever forget. You're no longer innocent. You pulled the rope."

Carlos's cheeks burned.

"Go pray," Estancia said. "Ask the Virgin Mother for her blessings. Live a Godly life and remember this feeling. Don't ever come this way again. Maybe, in time, the Father will judge you a good man."

"I can only hope."

Estancia nodded. "*Yo espero también.*"

With that, he drove his diggers into the mustang's side. The horse snorted and trotted south through the pines.

Carlos sat there for a while and watched him go, trying not to think of that white face from his dream.

Scotty Milder is a writer, filmmaker, film educator in New Mexico. He received his MFA in Screenwriting from Boston University, and his short films have screened at festivals all over the world. His short fiction has appeared in such magazines as Dark Matter Magazine, Cosmic Horror Monthly, Dark Moon Digest, and anthologies from Dark Moon Books, Dark Peninsula Press, and others. He teaches screenwriting and film production at Santa Fe Community College and the University of New Mexico. He is also host of the "Horror from the High Desert" podcast and co-host of "The Weirdest Thing" history podcast with actor/theatre artist Amelia Ampuero.

One Cold Bitch

J. L. Royce

As summer waned you arrived: empty, lightheaded, having fasted and purged. The sedation left you giddy and carefree in your virginal white gown. You were shown to your pod, your pressure-reducing couch—your home for the next month—and then you were penetrated with clinical intimacy: NG, catheter, rectal collector. Penetrated everywhere—almost.

You closed your eyes: *Let it be done unto me...*

The attendant delivered the *coup de grâce*—light anesthesia and the hypnotic agent—then activated the trans-cranial cortical adapters.

Your metabolism slowed, your temperature dropped, your blood rushed to serve your laboring brain, its psychic turgidity. Your body, that annoying, needy baggage, was massaged and sustained; tended to but ignored. Eagerly you entered the virtual classroom, learning at ten times the pace of the conscious world. You were healthy, smart, and would graduate from medical school two years early, with half the student debt.

You won't feel a thing. Your body will drift—that's what they said: *You won't feel a thing.*

They lied.

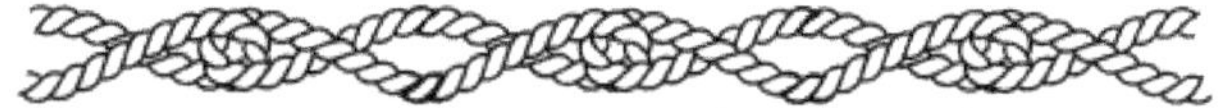

The visitor appeared in the late afternoon and paused in the open doorway. She was attractive and knew it, and knew Horace Smagele would notice. She stood in the intersection of natural light, warm and waning, with the cool, austere office lights.

"I haven't come for the marketing pitch." She glided into the director's office, swinging the door just hard enough to kiss the frame and close.

"You're renowned in hypersleep pedagogy. And of course, I'm already familiar with the Institute."

Smagele straightened and preened. "Indeed, I'm your man, Miss—" he glanced at his admin's hasty message on the tablet and cleared his throat "—*Doctor* Stanz."

"Please; Clarisse." She gestured at his open briefcase. "Were you on your way out?"

"Always time for an alum." He closed the case slowly, staring at it a moment before his smile waxed like a full moon over his desk.

Horace read on. "*And* you just graduated from Feinberg at Northwestern—congratulations."

The grave young woman approached his desk, descended into the guest chair, and placed her satchel close by her side: a large bag, professional, functional, ugly.

"What's your next stop, career-wise?" he asked.

"Residency at Johns Hopkins," Clarisse replied. "I intend to specialize in functional neurosurgery."

"Excellent, yes." Smagele (a mere Ph.D.) pursed his lips. "Well, Baltimore; but yes, I suppose the experience is worth it." He tapped a while on his tablet, nodding.

"So, you were a hypersleep premed—rigorous program, that."

"Yes; right here in Chicago, your facility."

Horace straightened his rumpled suit coat and leaned back to study his guest at leisure.

She sat quite erect, perfectly still, hands in her lap. Her suit was coal, the jacket open over a pearl-gray blouse sheer enough to distract. Her bobbed auburn hair glowed in the late afternoon sun.

Her only jewelry was a Medical Alert bracelet.

A rap on the doorframe jarred the Director from his contemplation.

"Dr. Smagele..." The admin frowned at the visitor, then smiled at her boss. "I'm leaving now—I'll lock up."

"Yes, yes."

"Can I get you anything? Or your guest?" She peered at the seated woman, who remained focused on Smagele.

"No!" Annoyance flickered across his face, chased away by a forced smile. "See you tomorrow."

Clarisse watched the woman retreat, then returned her gaze to Smagele.

His face was soft, his body heavy. Clarisse's mind wandered: *Smagele...smear.* Her vision blurred, his face seen as if through tears, becoming boundless: *a bulging blur—*

Horace cleared his throat. "I said—how can I help you?"

The young doctor struggled to focus. *Not tears—memories.*

"After my hypersleep, months later, I dreamed about it. About my time here, in your facility."

Horace gestured. "Given the manipulation of the diurnal cycle—eight-to-one acceleration—lingering sleep disruptions are an unfortunate—occasional—side-effect." He consulted the records displayed on his tablet before continuing.

"I see you finished the first year of pre-medicine before the holidays, returned after New Year's to finish your second year before spring, then the third year by summer. Three hypersleep shifts, back to back…"

He pursed his lips: *judgmental*. "We screen all candidates for epilepsy, neurodegenerative disorders, sleep disorders, of course—the results are in your file. Negative."

The pale blob waited for her confession.

"School was so expensive. I wanted the fast track so badly…I took anti-epileptics before the pre-admission sleep study."

Smagele stared at her, dripping sympathy, a steady seminal stream, warm and sticky: stared at his guest's angular face, the scissors of her crossed legs, the acute breasts.

Clarisse studied him studying her. "The dreams were vague for the longest time, twilight in a cold place, until my last year at Northwestern. I was rotating through EM—MVAs, gunshots, stabbings, rapes. The ED is the best place to hone surgical skills, you know, next to a battlefield triage. It was exhausting, but I was determined to succeed. Eighteen-hour shifts, napping in a break room.

"I woke up to the weight of someone on top of me, fumbling with my scrub pants, my underwear. Then he was inside me."

Her hand grazed her face: *no tears*. "Inside me. I could see his face, but blurred, just a round white blur."

Smagele straightened, his face melting in doubt disguised as concern. She imagined his inner monologue: *Didn't you scream? Didn't you fight? Did you* want *it? Isn't this* your *fault?*

Before he could protest, Clarisse said, "I couldn't move, I couldn't scream. I was paralyzed, in that half-sleep..."

"Hypnopompic state." His face bobbed, the moon's reflection rippling in a pond. "You were alone, imagined your assailant. Dreamed it."

"Yes! I knew you'd understand," Clarisse said, rolling out the tension in her neck. *Dreams...or* memories.

"I swore he was there, yet no one was seen entering or leaving. Nothing on security footage."

He nodded, and she imagined: *Just your hand, exploring your repressed needs.*

"I demanded a rape kit. Nothing. I had to admit... I had to accept..." She tried to focus on the blur sitting in the director's chair. "But it was so *realistic*; even the smell...his smell." Her nostrils flared.

"Fascinating," said Horace Smagele, with the clinical interest of an oncologist admiring a tenacious tumor. "I sympathize, but how can *I* possibly help?"

Clarisse Stanz locked her fingers around her crossed knee. "I was referred to therapy, as a condition of receiving my degree. Professionals in healthcare protect each other, you see; exhaustion, alcoholism, drug abuse...sexual abuse. Doctors help each other."

"Of course. Society expects so much of us."

"My therapist suggested a post-trauma pattern. We explored my childhood, adolescence—my family and friends—nothing. Which left one blank period, one gap."

Horace straightened in his chair. "You don't think something happened to you *here*?" A cloud eclipsed the moon-face. "Of course, I'll assist you if I can—"

"I'm sure you will." Clarisse smiled. "I've already made inquiries."

"Our hypersleep facility is under constant surveillance. I can retrieve the recordings—they're kept for seven years. Fully redundant system, hot spare. You could review your entire stay—however tedious."

Clarisse shook her head. "I imagine they'll show nothing." Her crossed leg bounced rhythmically. Her gaze drifted across the ceiling. "Paired cameras; the same image."

Smagele raised his hands in defeat. "I'm afraid you've lost me." He chuckled nervously.

"I asked a security expert about it. Two cameras, but only one recording is retained." Clarisse smiled. "Someone could set the timestamp of one camera a day earlier. After all, nothing ever happens in the sleep chambers; it's practically the same image."

"That sounds terribly complicated." Horace sighed: the wind distressing the moon's reflection. "But I can determine which technicians were on rotation during your—"

"I know; personal locators built in their IDs, with checkpoints around the sleep chambers. In my episodes, I heard a voice as well. When his hands were on me. He said *You're one cold bitch*."

She picked up her satchel and placed it on the chair. The latches snapped open with crisp clicks.

"I have the proof. When I take this to the authorities, your career will be over." Clarisse fumbled around in the depths. "I have it right here..."

"What proof?" Horace stood and leaned across his desk. "You have *nothing*."

"It's right here. The proof of what you did." She withdrew a sheet of paper and made a show of studying it. "I'll give you this one chance: prepare a confession, plead guilty, and agree to counseling. You might even avoid prison."

"This is outrageous." Horace stepped around the desk. "I admit nothing. You can't prove a thing. Show me!" He loomed over her, bending down to snatch the paper from her hand. She released it and he peered at the document.

Clarisse inhaled that familiar scent, from paralytic night-mares, and slowly raised her fist.

"What's this?" Horace frowned at it and mumbled, "A credit card bill? I don't—"

She jabbed the needle of the hypodermic into Smagele's fleshy upper arm and depressed the plunger.

He howled in surprise, reeling away from her. "What have you done?" He swayed and stumbled back, clinging to the desk, collapsing into his chair.

Clarisse unfolded her legs and stood. She said, "You're relatively healthy if a bit overweight. The succinylcholine shouldn't kill you—if I estimated your body weight correctly."

Horace snarled, tried to rise, swayed, and reclined, hard.

"I was going to include ketamine," she continued, "but that might dull your...sensations. Don't try to stand again; you could injure yourself. I wouldn't want to have to pick you up from the floor."

The angry moon-face blurred into soft complacency.

"That's right, relax," Clarisse said. "We need to prepare for the evening."

The big man sprawled in his chair, arms limp. He watched Clarisse lock the door, draw the blinds, and extinguish the overhead lights. The cold light vanished, replaced with the glow of his desk lamp.

"We have a few minutes before the paralytic wears off." Clarisse strolled around the office, unbuttoning her blouse.

"I don't want to get my clothes dirty," she explained. "Besides, I have no secrets from you...Horace."

Clarisse folded the blouse over the chair, then unzipped her skirt, and wriggled out.

"You might enjoy the evening more, this way."

She rummaged in her bag and brought out a roll of tape, a fluid bag with an intravenous set, and a collapsible pole. Next came nitrile gloves.

"I should be offended that you didn't recognize me. Of course, I changed my hair." Clarisse secured Horace's arm to the chair with surgical tape.

"No more *blonde ice queen.* Another term of endearment, wasn't it?"

She palpated his antecubital fossa. "Very nice," she murmured, her finger rolling the turgid vein.

She swiped the site with an alcohol pad. The needle penetrated. Clarisse adjusted the IV drip with practiced ease. "Just something to calm you."

Clarisse placed the mask on his face. She leaned close, nostrils flaring.

"I mentioned the scent, in the dreams." Clarisse closed her eyes. "Your scent. Soap? Body wash?

"I haven't done this before." She brought out the gas bottle, attached the hose to his mask, and opened the valve. "Oh, I understand the principles of anesthesia; but intentional induction of a persistent vegetative state without loss of spontaneous respiration..."

Clarisse chuckled to herself and sat down. "I love a challenge. And I'm confident my education prepares me for it. We'll just take our time."

From her satchel she extracted gauze squares, tape, and a dark bundle, cradling it a moment in her hand. Clarisse lay the prosection kit on Horace's desk, untied the faux leather case, and lovingly unrolled it to display the shining contents: scalpels, clamps, spreaders.

"Haven't used these since first-year Anatomy. Cleaned and sharpened—just for the occasion." Her fingers traced the first tools she'd employed in exploring the human mystery, in her quest to acquire the surgeon's skills, in those long hours spent disassembling corpses, with the patience and passion of a lover.

"The therapist insisted I 'confront my past trauma,' though I doubt she meant face to face." Clarisse laughed lightly. "I didn't share my theory with her. It does explain some of my...proclivities. But I won't bore you with details."

"I've imagined many endings to this evening—some of them quite extreme—but at what cost to my career?" She sat on the corner of the desk, crossing her legs and surveying her subject. "Should the punishment fit the crime?"

Her foot rocked gently as Clarisse relaxed and contemplated the moonrise in this, Dr. Smagele's twilight. The minutes ticked slowly away. She had almost dozed, so peaceful was this interlude.

Horace's eyes gleamed wetly—*was that a tear coursing down his cheek? Tears, on the moon?*

"How sweet...are you missing me already? Did you dream of meeting me again, as I've dreamed of meeting you?" Clarisse leaned forward "Don't worry, I'll come to visit you when you've settled into long-term care."

Her gaze wandered the room, searching the soft darkness filling the corners. "I recall something I read, that the heart can't stay away from that which hurt it the most. *A return journey to anguish...*"

Clarisse dared the room to refute her, but there was only silence.

"There's nothing for it, I suppose." She stood and stretched. The desk lamp set her body aglow, as it must have appeared in that dim sleep chamber. Stepping around the desk she unbuttoned Horace's shirt, loosened his belt.

Clarisse assumed the detached calm of the surgeon as she picked up her scalpel.

"It's late; we'd better get started."

J. L. Royce is an author of science fiction, the macabre, and whatever else strikes him. He lives in the northern reaches of the American Midwest, exploring the wilderness without and within. His work appears in Alien Dimensions, Allegory, Cosmic Horror Monthly, Fifth Di, Fireside, Ghostlight, Love Letters to Poe (Visiter Award winner), Lovecraftiana, Mysterion, parABnormal, Sci Phi, Strange Aeon, Utopia, Wyldblood, etc. He is a member of WWA, HWA, and GLAHW. Some of his anthologized stories may be found at: www.jlroyce.com.

Banks of the Laurel

D.L. Winchester

James Keith sat on his bed in the basement jail of the Madison County Courthouse. It was dark outside, the end of another long day waiting for his case to work through the justice system. The stone walls were cold, and the chill of the fall night permeated his small cell. His thin blanket helped, but it wasn't enough to beat the cold. Out the window, he could hear horses whinnying from the livery stable next door.

Damn his cousin! Lawrence Allen had only gotten a six-month suspension from the army for his role in the massacre, and now here Keith was being charged with murder! Two years had passed since Lee surrendered at Appomattox and Thomas surrendered the last of the Carolina boys. Far too late for charges relating to the war. It was hardly fair, but when the Yankees found out what happened at Shelton Laurel, Governor Vance needed someone to blame for what happened. Lawrence had always had better political connections, so Keith, his second-in-command, was taking the brunt of the persecution.

He heard the cellblock door swing open. The jailer was making his rounds. Well, it would be the same as it had been for most of the last two years. James Keith, alone in the cellblock, waiting for the State Supreme Court to rule on his appeal. As if what happened wasn't justified. The folks up in Laurel had taken to calling it a massacre, but it was a war, and anyone who wasn't willing to fight for the South was a traitor, damn it!

The cell door swung open, and a man appeared in the doorway. It wasn't the jailer. He was smaller than Keith, but his eyes showed the sharpness of a veteran, a man who had survived the scraps and skirmishes that marked warfare in the Carolina mountains.

"Colonel," the man nodded. "We need to move quickly."

"What?" Keith got to his feet. "Who are you?"

"My name is Pete. I'm here to bust you out. Our sources in Raleigh say the Supreme Court is not going to decide in your favor. If you don't come with me now, the only place you'll go is the gallows."

James nodded, stunned. No one had mentioned an escape attempt; he wasn't aware plans had been made. "Who sent you?"

"Is that important?" Pete pulled out a pocket watch. "I paid the jailer to take a ten-minute break. We're running out of time."

Colonel Keith stepped out of the cell and looked up and down the narrow hallway. Sure enough, there was no sign of the jailer.

"Quickly, Colonel," Pete said, leading him out of the jail and through a door to a narrow set of steps. Moments later, they were in the woods behind the courthouse, where a horse was waiting.

"We caused a problem out west of town to keep the sheriff busy," Pete explained. "The river road to Asheville is clear. From Asheville, you can take a train out of the state." He pressed some bills into Keith's hand.

Colonel Keith nodded. "How can I repay you?"

"Just go." He nodded toward the river. "Quickly."

Keith's horse trotted past the brick foundations of a ruined farmhouse, another casualty of the war. Keith pulled his cloak tighter around him. The night was dark, and the chill of the breeze off the river seemed to reach into his bones. It was twenty miles to Asheville, and as Pete had promised, the River Road was clear.

As he rode, he found himself angry again. Governor Vance wanted to hang him. The families of the Laurel community wanted the same. He'd seen them in the courtroom, their dark eyes filled with hatred. Given the chance, they wouldn't wait for the sentence to be passed, they'd kill him themselves. One of the women had slipped a note to his attorney as he left the courthouse.

It took eight shots for my David to die.

If I could, I'd give the same to you and your client.

They didn't, couldn't understand that the war was bigger than some dead men in a mountain valley. He'd done his part, done his duty, and the way he was being treated was wrong.

A light exploded from the road ahead, the sound of the explosion startling his horse and sending Keith tumbling off. Landing on the hard road, he lifted his head and watched the horse thunder away. Then strong hands were lifting him.

"You gonna go quiet, or'm I gonna have to make you quiet?" a voice whispered.

"Help!" Keith roared, a moment before he was knocked unconscious by a giant fist.

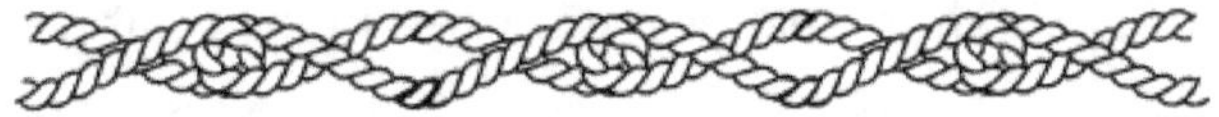

When he came to, he felt himself sliding. Looking to the right, he saw the lights of a town, and realized it was Marshall.

He was on the river.

Keith managed to roll over, and saw his captor standing at the back of the raft, a long pole in his hands. When he saw Keith was awake, he laughed.

"Enjoy your nap?"

For a moment, he didn't believe his eyes, but then a light from the town cast a beam out on the water. In the thin ray, the dark skin was obvious.

His captor was a Negro.

He was huge, a shadow that consumed the darkness behind them, powerful muscles pushing the raft along with minimal effort. The man talked like a local, but under the verbiage was the hint of an accent, a faint echo of the deeper south. It reminded Keith of the South Carolina and Georgia soldiers he had known during the war.

Keith tried to speak, but couldn't. A gag had been stuffed in his mouth, and his hands and feet were tightly bound.

"My name's Rufus," the man said, watching him struggle. "I'm sure that ain't what you want to call me right now, but that don't matter. Best you stay real still, wouldn't want you to fall in the water."

Keith tried to roll off the raft, but his captor reached out with the pole and smacked his head, making everything dark again.

When Keith woke up the next time, the raft was approaching a fire on the shore. There were men there waiting for them, and when they came close, some waded into the water and helped pull the raft in.

Rufus grabbed Keith and lifted him to his feet, then reached down and cut the cord that bound his legs.

"Everything go alright, Rufe?" one of the men in the water asked.

"Real smooth."

"Bring 'im up to the fire," someone called. "Let's get a look at 'im."

Keith's heart sank when he saw the people gathered around the fire. Men and women, the same men and women who had packed the courtroom for his trial. The leader was a smaller man, a vicious grin on his face.

"Hello, Colonel Keith," he said as Rufus brought him up the hill.

Keith froze. It was Pete, the man who had busted him out of jail hours before.

A woman came over, grabbing his face and taking a close look at it in the glow from the fire. "That's him, Pete," she said. "That's the one who had me whipped."

She was an older woman, perhaps fifty, with graying hair and fire in her eyes. Before anyone could stop her, she slapped Keith across the face, and Rufus let him fall to the ground.

"Easy now," Pete said. "The Colonel gonna get what he has comin' to him."

"Well hurry the hell up," another woman, this one older, called out. "I bin waitin' five years to see this man git what he got coming, and I don't want to wait much longer!"

Pete squatted next to Keith and pulled the gag out of his mouth. "You know why you're here, don't you, Colonel?"

Keith spit at Pete's feet, and the smaller man laughed. "That ain't nice, Colonel, but I reckon what you got comin' is a whole lot worse than a little spit. We heard a rumor the Supreme Court is gonna let you go, and that don't sit right with us. So we're gonna handle things the right way, make sure you get what you deserve." He looked at Rufus. "Get 'im up, Rufe."

Keith felt himself being lifted off the ground, but refused to stand on his own. A big hand held him by the scruff of the neck. "Don't mind holding you, Colonel. Don't mind one bit."

One of the women handed Pete a rope. "You remember this, don't you, Colonel?" Pete asked. "How you hanged the women, took 'em to the brink of death, then whipped them like dogs?" He tied a noose in the rope and put it around Keith's neck, then threw the slack end over the tree. Rufus took hold of the rope and pulled, lifting out the slack. He let go of Keith, who fell forward, the rope burning his throat as it stopped him from falling to the ground.

Around them, the men and women approached, clubs and whips in hand. A knife cut through the back of Keith's shirt, and the fabric was ripped away. The slack was pulled out of the noose, leaving Keith to stand on his tiptoes as the first man swung his club.

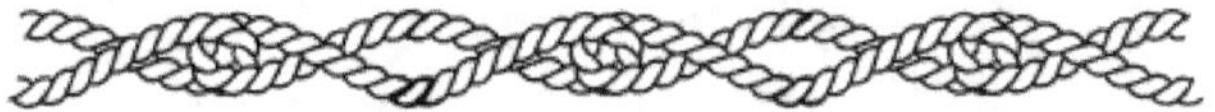

Keith regained consciousness as the sun appeared in the eastern sky. Pete was standing over him with the woman who slapped him.

"Reckon we ought to move things along," Pete said.

"I'd rather not, if it's all the same," Keith said, groaning as the pain radiated from his back through the rest of his body.

The woman shook her head. "Yo' debt has come due, boy. You took fifteen of our men and boys away to Knoxville as prisoners. Only thirteen didn't make it."

Pete nodded toward Rufus, standing at the edge of the crowd. "Rufus saw the whole thing."

Hearing his name, Rufus walked over to the prisoner. "That's right. You murdered all them defenseless men, even the boys. I'd just escaped, come north from near Savannah an' heard there was Lincolnites in Laurel. Got here to find the place crawlin' with Johnnies, so I hid out in the woods. Saw you bring the prisoners down the road, march 'em into the woods a few at a time, an' make your men shoot 'em. Lord knows your Johnnies didn't want to. You threatened 'em, told 'em you'd kill them instead. So they murdered all thirteen of 'em."

The big man was crying now, and one of the other men came and put an arm around his shoulders. "Wish I'd stopped you, but I was too afraid to. There was too many of you an' only one of me. So I waited 'til you moved on, then went on to the Laurel Valley. Found Pete here, an' we been workin' on gettin' justice for them boys ever since."

Pete smiled. "I came after you. Lord, I wanted some revenge, but though I got fifty-some men of your Sixty-Fourth North Carolina, I never got you."

The colonel's eyes went wide. "You're Pete McCoy!"

"That's right. I's one of the ones you captured, but a brother Mason helped me get away before the shootin' started. I ain't gonna be the one that finally gets you though." He took out a pistol and handed it to the woman. "This here is Ma Shelton. After you whipped her to an inch of her life, you killed her husband and her boys."

"The last one, the youngun', wasn't quick neither. Boy died beggin' for mercy," Rufus said. "He died with forgiveness on his lips, but you killed him all the same. That ain't right."

Ma cocked the gun. "Go to hell."

The bullet tore through Keith's gut, ripping holes in his intestines and starting a dark, bloody stain on his shirt. "You missed. By God, you missed."

"Didn't miss nothin'," Rufus said. "She shot you right where she wanted."

McCoy squatted next to Keith. "You see, here's the part you don't know. After your men did a half-assed job burying our boys, some hawgs came through and dug 'em up. By the time we found out what happened and got to the grave, they'd eaten on our boys for most of the morning." Pete shook his head. "Ugly sight, seeing them chewed up like that."

The sun had risen higher now, and a high squeal carried across the air. McCoy gestured to the creek running nearby that joined the river. "Colonel, you gonna die on the banks of the Laurel, just like them boys you murdered. Only you ain't gonna have to wait for them hawgs to get hold o' you."

Rufus lifted him off the ground and carried him toward a pit. The men and women took seats on the mounds of earth that surrounded it. As Rufus carried Keith closer, the squealing got louder.

"No!" Keith said, trying to twist free of Rufus. But the big man changed his grip, dangling the Colonel by his ankle, holding him out and away from his body.

Now Keith was dangling over the pit, the four hogs working themselves into a frenzy at the bottom of the eight-foot walls.

"Ain't been fed in two days," McCoy said, an evil grin on his face.

"Please," Keith stammered, "I'm begging you, show mercy."

Ma Shelton squatted so she could look into the eyes of the upside-down man. "We gonna show you the same mercy you showed my boy David." She looked up at Rufus. "Drop 'im."

D.L. Winchester lives in the foothills of southern Appalachia. A former mortician, his work searches the darkness to find tales worth telling. He is the author of over three hundred obituaries, numerous short stories, and the upcoming Flash Fiction Collection "A Terrible Place." In his spare time, he can be found searching for inspiration in the world around him and trying to keep his children from becoming the next generation of horror villains.

Passenger

J.B. McLaurin

George had never had much patience for the living. He'd always preferred the dead.

As a kid, Vale Cemetery was his favorite retreat, a place where he could be alone, free from the judgmental, small-town stares of the close-minded residents of Vale, Georgia. Over the years, not much had changed about the place. The boundary walls, made of large chunks of limestone, had more mold and moss covering them, and the gravestones were all shades darker from weather damage. For the most part, however, the haven of his youth wasn't worse for wear.

George was pushing forty, and though he'd left town years ago, attending college as far away as possible and then working in Atlanta as an IT specialist, he'd recently quit his job and moved back to his hometown. Reason being, his father had another stroke and couldn't care for himself.

His dad had been in bad health for a decade thanks to high blood pressure, high cholesterol, and a near-pickled liver. In the beginning, George's mom could still take care of him. That was back before the dementia started poking holes in her brain. She held on for as long as she could, even made it a few more years in a home, doing crossword puzzles—palliative care they called it—while she slowly forgot who she was.

His mom was buried in the new annex on the cemetery's north end. Her grave wasn't dark from moss and weather. It was only in its second year. Infancy for a gravestone.

Stuck in his hometown, suffering through the interminably long hours, George had fallen into his old routine of walking the grounds under the moonlight.

Vale Cemetery was a model of diversity when it came to headstones: unmarked, marble, concrete, tall, short, limestone, even the occasional obelisk. Some gravestones bore porcelain portraits of the deceased, which George found creepy. Not just because every stranger who walked the grounds could stare at the smiling faces of the deceased. That was plenty weird all on its own. What really bothered George was seeing the person as a living, breathing thing—bright, healthy, full of life. Then thinking about the current state of their body. Eyeless. Lipless. Decaying bones caked in mud. He didn't know yet whether he wanted to be buried or cremated, but his gravestone would state his name and the years he lived. No Bible verse. No uplifting quote. And absolutely no goddamn portrait.

A six pack of beer dangled from his hand as he walked between the tombstones. He'd spent enough time here to forsake the whole *don't walk on someone's grave* thing long ago. Somewhere in his teens, after he'd walked every inch of paved road snaking through the grounds, he started walking on the grass, right over the dead.

Around the same time, he got curious about the mausoleums and began going inside them when no one was around. Some of the tombs had nothing interesting to offer. Just dust, cobwebs, and an overpriced coffin. Others had all sorts of weird personal effects, like pins from Disney World or ancient books that looked like they belonged in an occultist's library. One even had guitars on display, strings orange from rust and holes in the body, where bugs ate through and made a hotel behind the pickups.

But, without a doubt, there was one he remembered above all others because of the town lore attached to it. Thrill-seekers had broken the lock off so many times the groundskeeper gave up repairing it. As a teen, he routinely went into the rectangular structure with Victorian gargoyles and angels on its eaves, but he'd never seen the fabled ghost. Not once.

Maybe this time would be different.

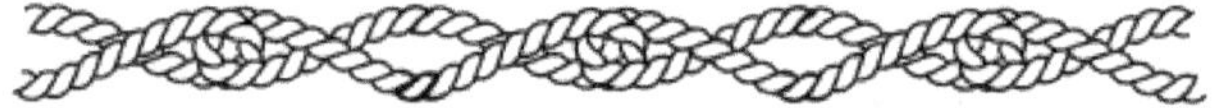

Inside, George admired the moonlit purple rose at the center of the stained-glass window on the mausoleum's back wall. Not even the heavy hand of time had diminished the beauty of the handmade window. Marveling at its elegance, his thoughts turned to the lore about this place.

The rumors about the ghost varied depending on which local was telling the story. Some said the ghost could time travel. Others said it could steal your soul. There was even an incantation, similar to saying Bloody Mary three times, that supposedly summoned the dark entity: *Come forth, oh dark one. Lift the veil between worlds and walk into ours.* George knew, firsthand, these words didn't summon forth shit. He'd chanted it hundreds of times, with not one damn paranormal sighting to show for it. One local, an artist, maintained the ghost could make you see into the mind of another. This artist had told the story while George was within earshot, as they were all downing beers at The Last Stop, Vale's working-class watering hole. The dimly lit, wood-paneled bar was a perfect spot to eavesdrop on drunk townies.

The artist claimed a childhood friend of his went into the mausoleum, saw some sort of humanoid-looking creature, and somehow ended up in another person's mind, like a passenger. George had overheard the story as he nursed beers at the bar. Dreading going home to change his father's diaper, he'd go there sometimes after he left the cemetery, fortifying himself for the night ahead.

Out of nostalgia, he whispered the incantation a few times—still didn't work worth a shit—then killed his fifth beer. Only one left. His head was swimming; the world had gone hazy. He thought of his father. He'd made sure he was asleep before leaving, but his dad often woke up needing water or a pain pill. George had been gone for two hours. Probably time to start heading back.

"Leaving so soon?"

George was buzzed, not drunk. He'd heard the question plain as day. But there was no one else in here to say the words.

Time to get gone.

He stood up.

"Leaving won't change your point of view." George spun in a half-circle toward the door thinking he'd see someone there.

"All of life, through the same eyes, informed by the same mind." The voice had a low tone, thick and sludgy.

George had experimented with every drug under the sun in college. Altering his consciousness had seemed like just the ticket at the time. He'd never much liked being George Chapman from Vale, Georgia and tripping let him leave himself behind. Vacationing in a dream world for a few hours brought him peace, but he knew it was just that—a dream. Part of him was always anchored to reality.

The voice he was hearing tonight was different. This wasn't the product of an altered consciousness.

This voice was real.

He turned around. Just above the rotting bench under the stained-glass window, something was flickering. Like an image on an old TV coming to life, starting as a thin staticky line, and then expanding, tearing a hole in reality as it grew and took form. Soon it was a large shadow shimmering like summer heat coming off asphalt.

Transfixed, George moved closer.

The shimmer took on a vaguely human form, almost like the creature was doing its best approximation of a person. Like it wanted to assume a form George's human mind could perceive and accept.

Within moments, a tall, man-like creature was sitting with his thin legs crossed like matching puzzle pieces. Smiling at George, he motioned for him to sit.

As he did, George's eyes never left the humanoid dressed in a fine suit; the thing was something of a neat freak; it flicked dust off its pants and even wet its finger to blot out a stain.

"Human consciousness is limited in so many ways. Don't you agree?" Eyes and mouth agog, George nodded. "Inability to see the whole color spectrum. Inability to see more than three dimensions. And how your kind struggles to think in the abstract. It must be quite frustrating, I imagine." George nodded like a congregant listening to a preacher. "But what has to be the most frustrating thing is living life from one point of view."

All the depression. The intrusive thoughts. Everything his mind had made him endure over the years. George had thought often about how nice it would be to have a fresh mind. One that wasn't always trying to turn the tide against him. And the only way to do it, to *really* do it, was to be someone else, inhabit a new point of view. *Otherwise, I'm stuck.*

"Or are you?"

Stunned, George said, "How did you...how did you do that? How did you respond to my thought like that?"

"Oh, George, do you really want to know?"

How in the hell does it know my name?

"Do you really think knowing will make you feel better?" The thing dusted off its pants again. "It's the mystery that's exciting, right? What fun is a magic trick once you know how it's executed? The mystery is what captivates the human mind. There's no solace in the answer, trust me. And besides, I didn't come here to give you answers, George. I came to make you an offer."

The creature talked fast, giving George no time to ask questions. Its offer: inhabit the mind of another human being for a brief interlude. But there were limitations. "You can't make choices for them. You can't influence their will. But you'll see what they see. Feel what they feel. Be privy to their thoughts. You will have the same point of view. Now you—"

"How long will I be—"

"George, I told you I didn't come here to give you answers. Don't interrupt me again." It was the first time George saw *it* angry. The thing's jaw tensed; little squiggly lines of veins poked out across his face, as if legions of worms were crawling under its milky skin. "There is one concession I'm willing to make: I won't put you in the mind of a child or a teenager. Your decades-old mind can't handle it. Too frantic." From thin air, a watch materialized on its wrist; looking down at it, the humanoid said, "You need to get moving. Time is short."

"So I just go out there, choose a name, and bring it back to you."

"That's right."

The thing had already explained George could choose the mind he would ride in. But the part that baffled George, that ripped away any shred of reality and made him think he was dreaming, was when the man-thing said he could only choose from those buried in Vale Cemetery. "But they're already dead."

"Your observational skills are second to none."

"So, what, I'm going to time travel?"

"If you don't believe me, you can walk back out and go care for your father."

More information that was impossible for it to know. *Was this thing omniscient? A god?*

"On with it. Go choose."

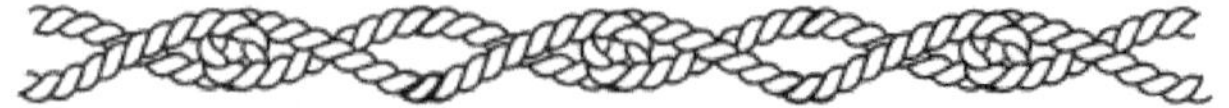

Before walking out, it told George he had half an hour to choose. With about seven minutes left, George had probably looked at thirty gravestones. For each one, he had some excuse to dismiss the person. *They lived too long. I only get one day. What if I get transported or teleported, or whatever, and it's their eighty-second birthday or something?* He needed someone that had lived into adulthood, preferably not past sixty.

Four minutes left.

Moving through the grids, the names and dates flew by: *Robert Mitchell, 1960-2011.* There didn't appear to be a wife or other family buried beside him. Maybe he was a loner like George. This guy was close, but not perfect. It had to be perfect. And for reasons George couldn't quite explain, he wanted to go further back in time. Maybe it wasn't enough to just live rent free in the mind of another. He wanted to experience a mind from a different era.

Two minutes left.

He ran farther back in the cemetery. After thinking he had found the perfect one twice, he settled on a candidate from the south corner. One of the older sections, but not the oldest.

George wasn't looking to end up in a Civil War battle. Just earlier in the twentieth century. A simpler time, as his dad liked to say.

"John Bradford. That's my pick."

"Are you sure?"

Absolutely fucking not. I'm still banking on the fact this is all a dream. But while I'm here in bizarro world, might as well take a shot. "As much as I'm ever going to be."

The thing smiled.

Then George's world, as he knew it, blipped out.

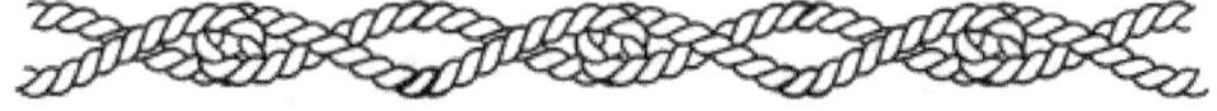

A diner. Pristine white table. Coffee cup just to the right of a plate of steak and eggs. Waitresses bouncing back and forth in dresses with wide trains like buttercups. There was even one of those tiny little jukeboxes on the table and the joint was packed with locals of all stripes: working class and business class hobnobbing before heading out to work.

Best George could place it: 1940s or 50s.

As promised, he looked out from a different perspective; the man's arms were shorter and hairier than his own. John also took his coffee black. As he sipped it, George felt the bitterness on his—well, not his, this guy's—tongue, reaffirming that he was a cream-and-two-sugars guy through and through.

At any moment, George believed the onrush of John's thoughts would come. A deluge of words, images, and sounds would flood his astral consciousness. Up to now, George hadn't experienced a single thought of John's. Either the man had no internal monologue, or something had gone haywire during his travel.

Sipping his coffee.

Steak and eggs untouched.

Not a single thought ran through John Bradford's mind.

It went on like this for fifteen more minutes, while John finished another cup of coffee. He didn't even speak to the waitress when she refilled the cup. Just a nod, then more sipping.

Growing bored as a spectator to a breakfast from a Norman Rockwell painting, George watched as John surveyed the bill, then left a tip.

John walked out to his Ford truck, glistening under the hot press of the Georgia sun. George could tell they were in Vale. He couldn't control John's movements—he had tried and failed to override the system and get a longer look at downtown. But he had seen enough on the periphery to recognize his hometown.

Leaving town, John lit a cigarette and turned up the radio. A tenor saxophone rang out from the shoddy speakers. When John finished one cigarette, he moved right on to the next.

His blank mental state continued. Maybe it was better to exist in a listless gray like him, George thought. Just drink coffee and smoke and blare jazz as the world lives and dies around you.

John parked the truck outside of a two-story rambler of a farmhouse. It had a large wraparound porch that George was admiring when the deluge of John's thoughts finally happened. It didn't come helter-skelter, thoughts bouncing off each other like moths crowding a porchlight, as George's mind so often did. Instead, there was a lone phrase—*It's time*—accompanied by a picture: an axe, with a clean brown handle and a gleaming blade, freshly sharpened.

As if he were watching a movie, George looked out of John's eyes while he walked to the back of the truck, robotically opened the tailgate, and took out an axe. The sharp edge sparkled in the sun.

A man appeared on the front porch. He stood over six feet tall, with wide legs under a beer-keg belly. "And how's my favorite stepson?"

George felt John bristle at the word *stepson*, then he felt John's abject hatred for the man—deep and all consuming, fire in his veins—take over.

"Don't come 'round enough. Hell, I was even starting to miss you." Acid drenched every word.

George heard that phrase again in John's head: *It's time.*

But there was more: *He deserves it. For what he did, he deserves it.*

As John walked up, dragging the axe behind him, letting the dry Georgia dirt speckle the blade, he began to replay a memory in his head. Captive, no ability to intervene or object, George watched:

A woman, maybe in her earlier thirties, blond and trim, getting thrown by a man so hard against a wall the plaster cracked. Next, the same man, dressed in overalls, threw her through a window onto the porch of this very house. She went through back-first; the panes splintered with a sickening crack; glass shattered in asymmetric pieces and chunks.

John, only ten years old, watched from the kitchen, while the man threw his mother through the window. He ran to check on her.

Her arms dripped with blood; shards of glass stuck out of her wounds like deformed teeth. John tried to ask if she was okay, but the man—who George now realized was the same man currently standing on the porch—thundered outside, picked him up, and pitched him down the stairs. John's left forearm snapped like a twig when he landed on it.

Then, the movie reel stopped, and they were plopped back down in the present.

No question, John's hatred for this man was beyond reproach.

"What you going to do with that? You never helped with a single damn chore while you lived here. Still got those twig arms. You couldn't heft that axe if your life depended on it."

John stayed quiet. They were eye to eye now. A nauseating cloud of dirt, vinegar, and blood wafted off the man; the smell of slow decay.

"What you doing here anyway, boy? I don't have time for this."

George felt John clench his jaw and widen his eyes, then say, "I know what happened to her now." The man clocked the axe, seeming to realize it might have another purpose today.

Waving his hand, he dismissed John. "She disappeared, boy. How many times do I have to tell you? Hell, how many times does the sheriff have to tell you?"

"For the last two years, she was right here, and I didn't know it."

"I ain't got time for this." The man turned to walk back in the house.

"Tanner!" The man kept walking into the house. "Tanner! You should read this." John reached into his pocket and pulled out what looked to be a letter. He threw it at Tanner's feet.

"What are you getting at boy?"

"Read it," John snarled.

Grunting as he reached down, back cracking, Tanner picked it up and started reading.

John waited a moment, letting his stepfather absorb the words: "You were drunk that night. You always were. Didn't have a sober day my whole childhood. That's why our farm died out. You had no discipline and damn sure didn't have any smarts." Tanner didn't respond; by the looks of it, he was too distracted by the letter to speak. "You thought if you took her out to the back of the property no one would see you." John moved in closer. "The sun hadn't quite come up that day, so you thought no one would be out in the neighboring field." He brought the axe around, gripped it with both hands. "Well, as with most things, you were dead wrong."

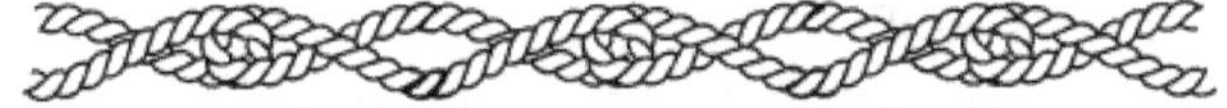

"Some farmers actually get up before sunrise and tend their land. And our neighbor, Mr. Patterson, was out there that day. You remember him, don't you?" At the sound of the name Patterson, Tanner looked up. "You hated him, remember? Because his mother was Indian. You always said he had dirty blood. Well, I guess the feeling was mutual. 'Cause just before he died, he sent me that letter." Clenching the axe tighter, John said, "He saw you dragging her body out there, then burying her. And he tried to tell your deputy buddies what happened. But they wouldn't listen to him. Because they were loyal to you."

Trembling, all the arrogance drained from his voice, Tanner said, "I'm done with this." He turned to walk into the house.

John whispered, "No you're not."

Shifting his weight, John moved the axe to his right, then side-swiped Tanner's right leg just below the knee, cleaving the lower half and leaving it looking like a cracked wishbone. Tanner crashed down on the porch, grabbing at his maimed leg. Chunky tendrils of gore and gristle spilled from the open wound; his lower-leg bones and foot dangled like a splintered tree limb. Screaming, writhing around in his own blood, he had gone white as moonlight.

"I always knew you killed her. Just like I always knew I shouldn't have left town for college." John didn't say it, but George heard the voice in John's head recall that his mother wanted her boy to go off to college and make something of himself. And when he had, the predator on the ground, currently rolling around and moaning, had moved in for the kill.

"Dammit boy, she left. She left!" Tanner yelped. "Get me some help. I'm bleeding awful! Get me some help!"

"You haven't checked on her in a while, have you?"

The question stilled Tanner. "You should have read that letter a little more carefully. Patterson told me where he saw you bury her." John reached in his pocket again and threw his mother's wedding ring—bearing her birthstone, an egg-shaped emerald—at Tanner. "I made sure she made it to the family plot, just like she wanted. She's buried by my daddy now. Like she always should have been."

With that, John didn't have anything else to say.

Tanner's face was the next thing he stove in.

All the years of having to listen to his stepfather's hatred and racism and rank idiocy had finally come to an end.

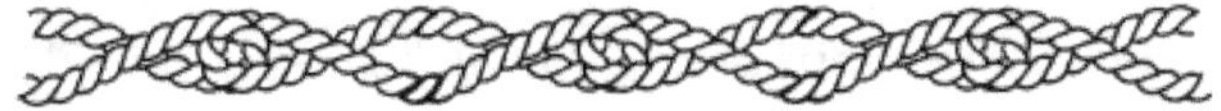

Under the cover of night, John moved the body—what was left of it—in a wheelbarrow. At first, George had no clue where he was taking the remains. As John pushed the wheelbarrow over uneven terrain, he didn't look down at his dismembered stepfather. George considered that a small mercy: he didn't want to see the severed limbs and entrails. He had already had a long, sickening look at all the pieces and bones as John packed them into the wheelbarrow.

John stopped at a corner of the fence at the back of the property. There was a row of dense pines on the other side of the fence, providing some privacy. John looked down at a hole in the ground that was relatively fresh. He had dug his mother out of it, under cover of night, and moved her to the family plot. This was the last part of his plan: burying his stepfather in this hole without a marker, uneulogized and left to rot without anyone knowing he was there.

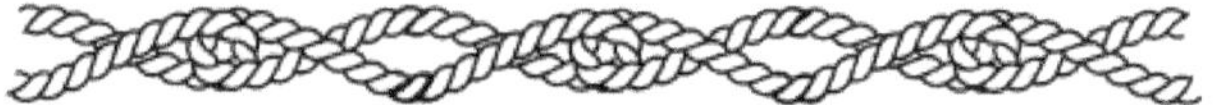

As soon as John's head hit the pillow, George snapped back into reality. He was back in the moonlit mausoleum, alone, with scores of questions. For instance, he wondered why John was buried in Vale Cemetery, not with his father and mother. He knew even if the humanoid that just gave him the ride of a lifetime had been there, it wouldn't have given him any answers. Like the creature said, it had come to give him an opportunity, not to enlighten him.

While he walked home, George thought about trying to track down the Bradford's farmhouse. Maybe go out and pay his respects to John's mother. Or maybe just see if the place even existed. Make sure it hadn't been a hallucination born from an overwrought mind.

After feeling the hatred John had for his stepfather, and seeing the domestic abuse that had torn John's childhood asunder, he was content to be back in his own head. He felt lighter. More at home in his skin than ever before. For the first time in his life, he thought maybe it wasn't so bad to be George Chapman from Vale, Georgia.

J.B. McLaurin obsesses over all things Stephen King and John Carpenter. He plays drums in alt-metal band Impossible Machine. Sley House Publishing released his novel *Black Echoes* last year. His story "For the Children" was published by Dark Lake in the *Theme is Revenge* anthology. Mobius Blvd. recently published his story "Covenant".

Erroneous Charge

Cyan LeBlanc

Sarah Roberts had never been with a woman before, though she had wanted to ever since she laid eyes on Whitley Blaylock.

Whitley was dark, mysterious, and captivating; not like other young women with their pink poodle skirts and light-blue sweater tops. Even Sarah dressed in the typical fifties fashion: a wasp waist with full skirt and a scarf tied around her neck. So when Whitley arrived in the small Midwestern town with her black hair and a wardrobe to match, eyes turned, and not in a favorable way.

Whispers began, especially when the town found out Whitley and another woman lived together. The other woman was older, and they looked nothing alike other than wearing black dresses that reminded folks of witches from a long-gone era.

Rumors flew.

Folks complained of pets going missing.

Livestock was found dead with their innards scattered in the field.

Although there was no proof the women were involved, the police had knocked on their door more times than not when someone filed a complaint.

It had gotten to the point that anytime Whitley came into the small downtown, folks dashed to the other side of the street to keep their distance.

Sarah, on the other hand, found herself drawn to the mysterious new arrival, like Whitley had cast a spell on her, a hypnotic desire that became an obsession. At night, Sarah found herself dreaming of this woman and touching herself while doing so. She had even gone to the town library, researching love potions and enchantments, which she tried at midnight when her household slept. During the day, this attraction had Sarah following Whitley through the town, hiding in the shadows just to get close enough to try to cast an incantation on her.

Each time, the words blew away in the wind, until the day Sarah had given up all hope of a charming the so-called witch. That's when Whitley startled her from behind.

"Why are you following me?" Whitley asked.

The words stumbled out. "I. Don't know. It's. You're so. I'm sorry. Go. Yes. I should go."

Whitley reached out and grasped her wrist. The gold flecks in her green eyes sparkled as she licked her lips. "Instead of going, you should come."

That was the moment Sarah believed her charms had worked. She followed two steps behind while glancing over her shoulder in case someone saw her traipsing through the poverty-ridden section of town with a so-called deviant.

The woman in black led her to the derelict house she shared with the other woman, who wasn't there when the two of them arrived. As soon as the door closed, as if possessed to comply, Sarah allowed Whitley to kiss her. With each lick and nip of her pale white skin, a layer of gooseflesh rose. Sarah's knees weakened as she moaned into every breath. She had wanted this since the moment she saw Whitley for the first time.

Now Sarah was on her bed, on her back with her legs spread wide, as if some unnatural force kept them pried open. When Whitley pressed her fingers into her molten sex, Sarah screamed from the pain. It hurt, though it was one of the best pains she had ever felt. Her body caved into it, wanting more. When Whitley repeated the motion, Sarah cried out again.

A door burst open. "Sarah!" A male voice called out. "Sarah, where are you?"

Both women jumped from the bed. Sarah grabbed her clothes with a whisper. "Shit. That's my brother. He can't see me—"

Jack stormed over the threshold of the bedroom, wide eyed as he witnessed Sarah covering herself. He held up the cross he wore around his neck, as if to ward off the devil. "Get away from her, you witch."

Whitley laughed, shaking her head at his words.

Instead of standing tall for her actions, Sarah rushed to her brother's side and clung to his body for protection. They backed out of the room; the cross guarding them from the impurities of the house of sin. Sarah buttoned her white blouse and straightened her scarf behind her brother's back as he stood as a shield.

"How did you find me?" Sarah asked.

They stepped from the house. "My friends said they saw her grab you next to the post office, and next thing they know, you're following her to this God-forsaken place. I'm glad I saved you before she could sink her teeth into your flesh. We'd have lost you to evil."

Sarah couldn't tell the truth. She couldn't say she willingly offered herself to Whitley, a decision she would repeat without hesitation. It was easier to say Whitley seduced with her wicked ways than to allow the town to shun her.

At her brother's side, she listened to Jack jabbing her with insults about how susceptible she was to the powers of the dark witch. She said nothing. Her tears held more words: ones that were misconstrued as a violation by a vicious nymphet.

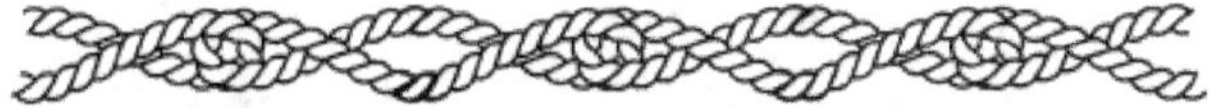

Over the next few days, Jack's discovery of Sarah in the witch's lair turned into a feeding frenzy of rumors. Most of which was ignored by Sarah. Her silence seemed to fuel the imaginations of her brother's friends. This raced to their friends, and so on. It wasn't like she could tell them it was a lie, that she willingly went with Whitley back to her home and removed her blouse and knickers without even being asked.

Jack might have discussed her encounter with the town's outcast among his friends, but he kept silent around their parents. If they knew, she most certainly would have faced exile in the asylum, where they sent all the victims who had succumbed to the devil's playground. Neither Jack nor Sarah wanted that to happen.

Instead, Jack and his buddies gathered one rainy night in the basement of an abandoned church to discuss the situation.

"This witch has gone too far, bringing an innocent girl toward Satan's ways. Something needs to be done about this," Jack opened the meeting with fourteen others sitting in a circle of chairs, as if this was an official meeting of the minds.

"Jack, please. I'm fine. Nothing happened," Sarah pleaded, trying to stop the growing tension in their voices.

"Shush. That woman put you under a spell. No woman of God would engage in such unholy acts if not for the wicked. This is why you're on your knees, praying for the Lord to expel that demon from your soul." Jack returned his attention to the others. "Now, I fear for the other women here. I fear for our sisters and mothers. Yesterday, I spoke to Preacher McCarthy, and he was no help. Temptation is a sin, though not illegal, so they will not lock her up for her crimes."

"Maybe she's fled the town. I haven't seen her wandering the square lately," Melissa, the sister of Jack's best friend, Brian, said. "It's possible she knows we're onto her and her witchcraft."

Brian shuffled in his chair. "No. She's still there with that other woman. I've seen them through the window. I wonder what they do in there all the time?"

"Sex. Perverted sex games. Plotting to seduce and kidnap the women of this town," Jack said.

"Jack!" Sarah exclaimed. "That is not true."

"I heard from Mary Beth, who was told by a friend's cousin, that those women cast a spell on them and made them bark like dogs with a snap of a finger," another girl from the circle stated.

"That is crazy. They wouldn't do that. No one could do that," said Sarah, debating the lies being spouted.

Jack stood, walked over to Sarah, and reached his hand out for her to take. "You're not well. You don't have a good head right now, because the witch has poisoned you. Go home and let us decide what to do about this woman. Go home and pray." He picked her up from the chair, turned her, and shuffled her out the door.

As soon as the door closed behind her, Sarah put her ear to the door to hear Jack voice his plan. "It's our job to see that she is prosecuted for her crimes against decency. If the police will do nothing, we must take matters into our own hands."

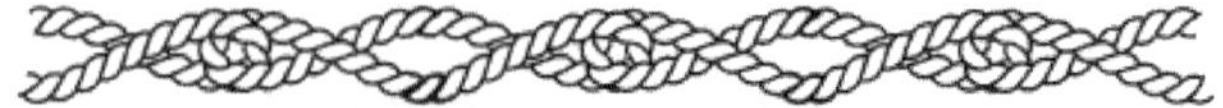

Sarah ran in the rain toward Whitley's house. She had only been there once and hardly remembered the route they took when they walked together. It wasn't the pristine streets of ranch homes, but the broken cobblestones of old, weathered homes that had been left abandoned. As long as the dwellers remained peaceful, the police let them squat. Whitley didn't look like her homeless neighbors with rotten teeth and body odor, but she lived in the same area as them.

Turning at a familiar-looking corner, she came upon the house. The blackened door, charred as if consumed by flames, hung loose on its hinges from Jack's previous intrusion.

Sarah knocked. The door leaned in even more, hanging on by its last screw. "Whitley?"

The other woman peeked through the crack in the door. "You need to go. Leave us be."

"I need to talk to Whitley. Please."

Just then, Whitley pushed the woman aside and pulled the door open, stepped through it and then closed it just as quickly. "Sorry. My sister is very protective of us. I never thought I'd see you again. At least at my house." She smiled.

It was caring and loving, and everything that had brought Sarah to her knees once before. If it wasn't for Jack's persistent talk of vengeance, she might have leaned in and kissed Whitley on the lips, which seemed to have a darkness like she painted them with charcoal gray lipstick. Instead, she was at a loss for words.

"I'd invite you in, but the last thing I need is—"

Sarah broke into Whitley's sentence, unable to control the urge any longer. She leaned in and kissed her, taking all her words and sucking them down into her lungs. When they parted, Sarah had forgotten why she had come all this way.

Whitley nudged her away. "You should go. As much as I want you to stay, you need to go."

With that, Sarah stepped from the rickety porch. The rain had quit, and she began her trek back to her home on the other side of town. Her head was in the clouds the entire way, forgetting everything she had wanted to tell Whitley.

It wasn't until she saw Jack and his gang of vigilantes storm from the church into the empty town square wearing black robes and plastic Halloween masks that she remembered. While Sarah could not see their faces, she knew them and watched their determination as they marched together down the cobblestone street.

"Jack. Stop!" Sarah pleaded as she turned and followed. "Don't do this."

Each member of the mob had weapons, equipment found in the church's basement like shovels, rakes, and pitchforks. One lit a torch, illuminating a path where no streetlights reached. With each step forward, Sarah attempted to stop them. Begging and screaming, hoping someone would come to her aid.

"Please, Jack! Stop. It was me. I did this. Don't hurt her. She's not a witch. Witches aren't real. Stop! Jack!"

The pleas fell on deaf ears.

With every ounce of energy, Sarah sprinted ahead of them, hollering at the top of her lungs. "Whitley! Whitley!" The crowd wasn't far behind her when she bound up the stairs and banged on the door. "Whitley, open! Please open the door!"

As soon as the door opened, Whitley's eyes widened in horror. The riot turned the corner with their pitchforks in the air. Anger mobsters waved bats and shovels, chatting with each step. "Burn the witch!"

The house wasn't safe. With its weathered wood, it would be easy to break down. The street was a dead end, with nothing but woods beyond it. Their only other option was to duck between the houses and over chain-link fences to get back to town, but there was no certainty they'd be safe.

The entire situation was surreal, unbelievable that a group of people were mad enough to believe in Halloween stories and the folklore of ancient times.

"Burn the witch! Burn the witch!"

When the cloaked clan showed no signs of stopping, Whitley took off, sprinting into the woods. They picked up their pace, charging after her, hollering with their weapons in the air. "Get her! Let's burn her at the stake!"

Just then, Whitley's sister bolted through the open door. "What's going on?"

Sarah had just leaped from the porch, her heart pounding in her chest when she hollered back, "They're going to kill Whitley!"

The two of them chased after the rioters, hoping to stop the determined, self-appointed bounty hunters, ducking into a dense grove of trees that provided a maze of confusion, and a possible escape for Whitley. No matter how much Sarah wanted to be with Whitley, she needed her to flee if she wanted to live. Only once had Sarah been in these woods, and she would have been lost if it weren't for her brother and his friends. What she knew was if they headed north, they'd run into the unmarked graveyard. People buried the destitute and homeless with no distinguishing markers, except for makeshift crosses fashioned from wood scraps or sticks.

After a bit of zigzagging, and stumbling over the thick tree roots, Whitley's sister tugged Sarah's arm and pulled her back. They listened to the woods. Commotion started up to their left, and they hurried in that direction, following the growing sound. Voices, loud, chanted. "Burn the witch! Burn the witch!"

Upon reaching the open brush, the two women discovered Whitley bound to a tree. Sarah froze, paralyzed in terror at the sight of twigs, sticks, and branches surrounding Whitley and this mighty tree. This was their stake, and Brian dropped the torch onto the pile of rubble. With little rain, it blazed in a matter of seconds. While Whitley tried to scream, the rope muzzled her and muted her cries.

As the sister rushed forward, Jack smacked her with his shovel. She tumbled into the fire. It caught her dress, also black as soot, igniting it. She tried to stand, screaming into the darkness, and attempting to snuff out the flames.

Jack walked over to her, calm, as if evil himself. He raised his shovel as he called out, "Sinner!" and slammed it into her face. She stumbled again, falling unconscious.

Melissa, behind Sarah, whispered in her ear. "Our own little witch trial, isn't it fun? Historical."

The words acted as a catalyst, unearthing long-buried thoughts and feelings inside Sarah. A powerful rage erupted from the pit of her stomach, surging electricity through her veins and out her fingertips. Her hands tensed and rose into the air, taking the fire away from Whitley. Flames danced in the air, whipping toward the spectators, who stood wide eyed and frozen in horror. One by one, bursts of fire engulfed them. Skin charred, then melted away from bone. Some fled in terror as others withered away into a puddle of ooze seeping into the grass.

Sarah did not release them. No, she transformed the blaze into Satan himself. He laughed as Sarah grabbed each of the deserters by a magical force and tossed them through the air into Satan's infernal playground. And once she had wrangled every one of them, she closed her fingers that diminished the fire god into a kindling of smoke.

Looking away from the aftermath, Sarah glanced up to see Whitley still bound to the tree. Her face was white. Horror and fear had drained her soul. Sarah rushed to her, knocked aside the burnt and smoldering brush. As soon as she touched her, Whitley flinched, though Sarah didn't let that stop her from tearing at the ropes, loosening them until they fell from around her. They stood there, staring at each other.

"You're a witch," Whitley said, so soft that alone the breeze heard and carried it away.

"Are you afraid of me?" Sarah asked, dropping her head as if this realization caused her shame.

"No. I think I love you more." Whitley reached up, grabbed Sarah's cheeks, and pulled her in for a breathtaking kiss.

Cyan LeBlanc is a queer novelist who began writing in 2008 in a wide variety of genres including romance, erotica, thrillers, and most recently, horror. They've focused solely on writing Sapphic (lesbian) characters and stories, but there's always an underlying love story, even when the main character is a flesh-hungry cannibal. Currently, Cyan lives with their wife and two furriors (cats) in Houston, Texas.

Death is Different
Tommie Simmons

"We have no way of judging how many innocent persons have been executed, but we can be certain that there were some."
– United States Supreme Court Justice Thurgood Marshall, *Furman v. Georgia* (1972)

Everything seemed fine with Alissa Usher until about a year after Vince Welch's execution. I'd seen her shortly after the execution–she'd had me over for lunch since I was in Idaho for a work conference–and she'd been fine then. Or seemed fine.

Whatever conversation we had about Vince Welch and his execution, she'd ended it the way she always ended conversations about her work as an attorney in the capital habeas unit. She was spending the best years of her life on endless appeals of death sentences, but she was always laconic about it.

"Death is different, Zena," she'd said, setting down a cup of tea on the dining room table she'd just cleared from lunch, her eyes on the birdfeeder outside her window. "It just is."

I'm still not sure what it means, but then again, tax law is about as far as you can get from capital habeas cases. I wasn't expecting to know. After all those years, though, I could hear subtle differences in the way she gave me that same enigmatic answer.

Sometimes, it seemed to me, in reference to certain cases, she believed it more. Sometimes death really was different from other defense work in a way that left her a changed woman.

Other times, it was just criminal defense. And sometimes in criminal defense, you lost.

Or at least, that's how I took it, having never wanted anything to do with criminal defense. I knew Alissa well though, and she'd talked about this type of career going all the way back to our first year in law school. I could tell–or at least, I used to think I could tell–when she believed a death penalty case was different from any other case.

When she really was going to lose a piece of herself on it.

The way she said "death is different" on that June day in her Victorian living room, I would have bet Vince Welch's case was not one she'd take to her own grave.

I certainly felt like the Pacific Northwest was better off without a serial killer and rapist. I didn't mourn his 20-year killing career, only the 13 women we knew he'd raped and killed, and the many more we didn't know about. Between everything Alissa had told me about the case and everything I'd read in the news, I felt OK about the Idaho Department of Correction shooting Welch's veins full of poison. He was the reason women like Alissa and I couldn't walk home alone at night.

It made sense this execution wasn't one she felt really bad about.

Again, though, it wasn't like we talked about it at length, so I'm mostly speculating here. That afternoon, I was just glad to see she looked like she was holding up all right and glad we got a chance to meet up. I was mostly disappointed Byron was working that weekend, so I didn't get to see him too.

Byron started texting me eight or nine months after that visit to Idaho. I was back in Denver then, and I hadn't had a reason to get back up to Idaho. At first, I was glad to hear from him; the three of us had been close when Alissa and I were in law school, and we didn't keep in touch enough.

But he made it clear he didn't just want to shoot the shit.

"Have you heard from Alissa lately?" He asked after we'd gotten through the hey-how-are-yous.

It seemed like an odd question. Surely, he didn't need to go around asking his wife's friends who she'd been talking to?

But I had known him for a long time, and I trusted him.

"I haven't checked in for a while," I admitted. "Is she...is she all right?"

I hadn't heard from Alissa, not since we'd gotten lunch together when I'd been in Idaho. He didn't say why that mattered, not then. But he did keep texting me, checking in, as if comparing notes. And gradually, I started to realize he had concerns.

It started with him seeing Alissa less. She'd go to work, come home, and lock herself in her office, or sometimes, Byron told me, her workshop. This wasn't necessarily weird: Alissa had studied engineering in undergrad, and sometimes her idea of a fun Friday night was locking herself in her workshop and making odd little contraptions. I told Byron she'd always been that way; in law school, I'd go over to her apartment only to find it strewn with tiny gears and springs.

But Byron was persistent. By May, he wasn't seeing her much at all, maybe a few times a week. By June, she'd started communicating with him by text, because she stayed in the workshop in the basement and kept the door locked.

That wasn't like Alissa.

About that time, I started calling her too. I'd been texting her all spring, since Byron reached out, trying to skirt the edges of whatever was going on, coax out an answer without upsetting things between us. But now I was worried.

I called for the first time in mid-June, my hands shaking, palms slick with sweat.

I've never liked confrontation, I guess. It's why I went into tax law.

She didn't pick up.

She texted me about an hour later apologizing, saying she'd been working late.

And it went on like that for another three weeks. Alissa was working late. Alissa had had a doctor's appointment. Alissa had had a board meeting for the local historical preservation society.

I relayed full, dutiful accounts of my efforts back to Byron. And *we* called each other, for all the good it did.

In the end though, that proved to be not much. By August, she'd told him she wanted a divorce, speaking to him in person for the first time in weeks. He'd moved out by the end of the month.

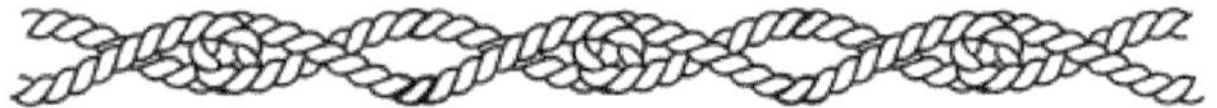

It was actually Alissa's idea for me to come visit her in September. She sounded different when she called. Unwell. I wasn't sure if it was a bad phone connection or if she had taken up smoking again. Regardless, I was worried. And glad she wanted help.

September in Boise is unbeatable, everything I'd always wanted from fall in Denver and never quite got: air so crisp and brittle you feel you could reach out and snap it apart; trees alight with a bouquet of fiery colors set against a cloudless cerulean sky; the faintest of breezes with only a nip of something colder, something darker on its hems. I'd spent the flight out feeling, by turns, sick to my stomach and hopeless despair: I didn't know what was happening to Alissa and I wanted to be ready for the worst. Ready for some sort of civil commitment hearing or something if necessary. Byron and I had talked, but not much; we'd both wanted to keep this on Alissa's terms as much as possible, to not betray her trust any more than we had to.

Stepping into the city, into that dream of an early-autumn afternoon, I felt better. Maybe this wasn't totally fucked. By the time I got to Alissa's front porch–piled high with drifts of yellow leaves–I was even looking forward to this.

One look at her face when she answered the door turned my stomach to ropes again.

She'd lost weight. She'd always been healthy, but not any-more; she looked gaunt, and at least five years older than when I'd seen her last year. There were new, deep lines on her face, and her hair was longer–and shot through with more gray–than I'd ever remembered before. Her eyes darted back and forth like those of a small, trapped animal as she opened the screen door to let me in.

Her voice was the same though.

"Zena," she said, stepping back into the entryway. "Thank you so much for being here."

"Of course," I said, hoping I'd hidden my surprise.

I hugged her, and felt bones in her back and sides I'd never been able to feel before.

I forced a smile, held her at arm's length.

"It's so good to see you," I said. "How are you holding up?"

She shrugged, and a sallow smile crossed her lips. Her teeth were yellower than I remembered.

"Oh, you know," she said, and looked up, through her dining room window, at the birdfeeder. "Things have been...different lately."

"Yeah," I said, as I took a seat at the dining room table and watched her shuffle to the kitchen to get me a cup of coffee. "That's what it sounds like."

I swallowed hard and now I felt sick again. Alissa was in her early 40s. She moved and acted like she was twice her age.

"It's been weird, not going into work as much," she said, as she returned to the table with two cups of coffee.

I nodded but didn't say anything; she'd mentioned she'd taken a bit of a hiatus from work.

She raised her coffee cup to her lips, eyes on the birdfeeder outside.

"I'm rethinking this job for the first time since leaving law school," she said, and sighed. "Death is different."

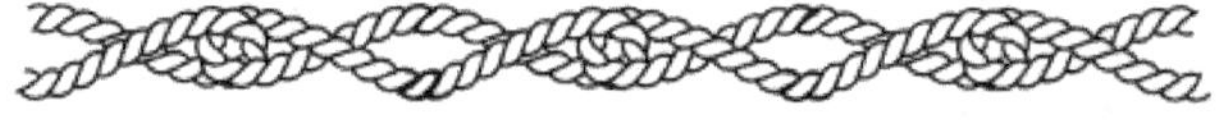

Alissa's house creaks at night. I wasn't surprised by that, given its age and location in the foothills, but I realized that night I'd never actually stayed the night there. Nor had I ever been inside the guest bedroom.

It was a small, well-furnished thing, the kind of cozy room you often find in 19th century homes. It occupied one of the house's turrets, and had a hexagonal feel to it. A floor-to-ceiling bookshelf took up the wall opposite the bed, near a window looking out over the foothills to the north, and the distant, jagged peaks beyond that.

Coming back into the bedroom after brushing my teeth, I paused in front of the bookshelf and examined the titles.

Some of them I expected. There were books of caselaw, biographies of famous Supreme Court justices, and more than a few tomes written about the death penalty through the ages. Others made more sense after I thought about it: books about science and engineering, one or two about physics. Alissa was one of the few people I knew who had studied the hard sciences in undergrad. She'd always had a gearhead streak, but now I gave these titles an extra look, remembering Byron's account of Alissa spending more and more time in her workshop, eventually never leaving.

Towards the bottom shelf, one dog-eared book sat cocked at an angle from the others, slimmer than the others as well. I bent to look at it; sticky notes flapped against my fingers as I flipped through the pages.

It was a biography of Thomas Edison. Someone–and I recognized Alissa's handwriting–had scrawled notes in the margins and highlighted paragraphs here and there. I paused at one particularly marked-up chapter titled "The Quest for the Electric Chair."

I blinked. I'd had no idea Edison had been instrumental enough in the creation of the electric chair to warrant a chapter in his biography.

A true intersection of Alissa's interests.

I paused and cocked my head.

I couldn't place what I heard, but it wasn't just the creaking and settling of the house. I furrowed my brow, then crept toward the closed door and held my breath.

It sounded like a cat, lost in the throes of a mournful, almost-human keening. The yowl went on for a few seconds, died away, and then picked up again: same wailing notes, same rise and fall, followed only by silence.

I opened the door as quietly as I could, still not breathing.

It gave onto a small upstairs hallway. A railing separated me from the dining room below, where Alissa and I had had dinner earlier that evening.

I cast a glance down the hall, in the direction of Alissa's room, and my heart leaped into my throat.

Suppose I found the door open and the light on, the window broken and her bed empty? Suppose I glimpsed the slow, sickening spin of her body as she hung from the ceiling? Suppose—

But I saw only the closed door, and there was no light in the thin space between it and the floor.

Below me and beneath me—meaning, somewhere in the far reaches of the parlor one floor below or, more likely, just outside that room's window—the cat started up again, its thin wail rising like candle smoke in the big, dark emptiness of the house.

I shook my head, cast one more glance toward Alissa's door down the hall, and headed back to my room.

She was up before me the next morning, sitting at the dining room table and sipping coffee, eyes on the dining room window and the autumn morning sunlight streaming in. I smelled eggs and toast and heard birdsong through the windowpane.

"Morning," I said.

She blinked and looked up at me. "Good morning, Zena. Breakfast is on the stove."

I nodded and made my way into the kitchen. A skillet of fluffy scrambled eggs sat on the stove and two slices of sourdough bread reposed on a plate nearby.

However bad Alissa might be doing, she still had the capacity to put together a good breakfast.

"Thanks so much, Alissa," I called back to her. "This looks great."

I scooped up some eggs, waited a moment for the toast to finish, and then headed back into the dining room.

She had eaten too, I noted, which I figured was another good sign, even if she still looked like she hadn't slept the night before.

"Well," she said, and set her coffee cup down on the table as I approached. "I'm feeling a bit better today. I don't know if it's just having you here or what, Zena, but I really appreciate it. I think I'm going to try to get some work done."

I took a bite of egg. I hadn't expected this at all.

"Are you sure?" I asked, then caught myself. "I mean, that's great if you're feeling up to it–really, it is–I just want to make sure...it's what you want to do. You said you had some time off?"

She nodded. "Yeah, they've been really good about this whole thing. Told me to take a while. But I want to get back into it."

She paused, shifted her utensils on her plate.

"I haven't taken the lead on a new case since Vince Welch's execution," she said. "And that one..."

She sighed. I waited, pursed my lips, and wondered if I should say something, but still wasn't sure what, exactly, would be good to say.

"That one still kind of bothers me, you know, Zena?"

I sipped my own coffee and nodded.

"Yeah, Alissa," I whispered. "I bet it does."

It was a lie. I had forgotten about Vince Welch's execution altogether; I was surprised it was still on Alissa's mind at all.

"There were some things..." she said, and paused, tracing an invisible pattern on the tabletop with one fingernail. "There were some things about that case I would have done...differently."

I reached across the table and put my hand on hers, stopped its movement.

"That was more than a year ago, Alissa," I said. "And you did all you could. I know that because I know you. I know how you believe in this work and how you care about clients. I thank

God for people like you, because I don't know anyone else who could defend these people. And it's *needed* work. Whatever happened with Vince Welch is in the past."

She sipped her coffee, kept her eyes on the birdfeeder, and said nothing. I'd spoken too much; I could tell by the few rapid blinks she gave, biting back tears.

It wasn't until I was about to go into Boise for groceries that I remembered my question for her, from last night. I thought it might cheer her up, might offer a momentary distraction from whatever she was reliving about Vince Welch's execution.

"I didn't know you had a cat, Alissa," I said, and forced a smile. "Is that new?"

She tore her eyes from the window; they were dry now. Her brow knit in confusion.

"I don't have a cat," she said. "What do you mean?"

The house was empty when I got back. Or at least, I didn't see Alissa in any of the common areas.

I climbed the stairs to the second floor. The bathroom was open and empty, and Alissa's bedroom door was also open.

The room inside was empty, I could see even before I alighted into the hallway.

I cast a glance over my shoulder and then back into the room.

I felt gross for even thinking about what I was thinking about. But Byron had told me he was worried about Alissa and anyway, I was worried too. It was enough to force me across the threshold into my friend's bedroom.

Everything looked to be in order. She'd made the bed, the floor was clean, the vanity in the corner looked well-kept. The bedside table –

I paused; my gaze snagged there for a moment.

The Thomas Edison biography from the guest bedroom sat on the bedside table. I'd left it on my own nightstand when I'd come down for breakfast that morning; I remembered that distinctly.

I took a step forward, toward the bedside table, then paused.

A scream ripped the house's silence apart. It sounded muffled—coming, maybe, from the direction where the cat's yowling had come from last night—but I still heard it.

And it shot my blood full of ice.

I grabbed the book and tossed it into the guest bedroom on my way down the stairs.

In the dining room I froze and realized I didn't know where Alissa's workshop was. I swallowed hard, caught my breath, and tilted my head to listen.

From somewhere in front of me and below me I heard the sound of machinery: metallic squeaks, pneumatic hisses, and something else I couldn't quite place. Something muffled.

I moved through the dining room, past the table, past the window and the birdfeeder away to my left, into the kitchen.

Nothing seemed out of place here; I saw the dishes drying in the rack just as I'd left them after breakfast, before I'd gone for groceries.

I made my way through the kitchen, into the hallway behind it. A century ago, this would probably have been where the house's staff would move dishes out of the kitchen to the rest of the house, but now it sat empty and dusty.

With a closed door at one end.

I moved closer to that door, paused when I was maybe a few inches from it.

The sounds were louder here. The machine – whatever it happened to be – was working faster now. I could pick out the mechanical grind of gears and the squeak of what sounded like a car engine with the key turned too far in the ignition.

I put my hand on the doorknob. It turned.

A set of wooden stairs descended into darkness before me. I took a step down, paused, then took another.

Something creaked in the semidarkness ahead of me. I cocked my head, took another step.

It wasn't until I saw Alissa's shoulder that I realized she was hanging from the ceiling.

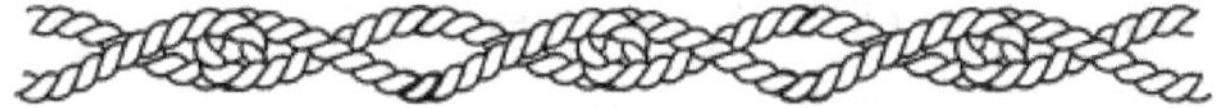

I opted to stay at the house that night. I got back late—Alissa was still in the hospital, comatose, and Byron was there with her—and by then I'd talked to so many cops and paramedics and nurses that all I wanted was some damn peace and quiet. I picked up a bottle of whiskey on the way home. I don't drink much but I wanted something to take the edge off.

I got to the guest bedroom, closed the door behind me, and poured myself a few fingers.

The Thomas Edison biography was still on the bed, where I'd thrown it when I'd heard Alissa scream. I cocked my head at it, confused.

I had forgotten all about it until now.

I set the whiskey on the bedside table and picked up the book again. I'd marked the chapter about Edison's work on the first electric chair, but there was another chapter dog-eared closer to the back.

I flipped to it. The information on the page didn't register for a moment.

This chapter was about Edison's efforts toward the end of his life to build a "spirit phone" that could communicate with the dead.

Alissa had marked up these passages even more than those on Edison's work on the electric chair. There were notes and highlights here, most of which I couldn't read, some of them ending in question marks. Whatever she'd been thinking about, she'd had a dialogue with this chapter, had proposed ideas and checked them against what she found here.

"What were you up to?" I whispered.

The keening started up again then. It still sounded animalistic and tortured.

I remembered the look on Alissa's face when she told me she didn't have a cat.

And what's more, I was pretty sure I could place where that sound was coming from now.

I was pretty sure it was coming from Alissa's basement workshop.

The sound rose again, one piercing, mournful note, before it dipped, seemed to get quieter, but not quite fade away.

I froze, then set the book down on the bed.

Alissa hadn't awoken since I'd found her hanging, so there was no way to know what, exactly, she was working on in the basement.

But she had been working on something; that much was apparent. I hadn't thought about it since getting her to the hospital, but thinking about it now, I could see the workbench strewn with tools, metal parts, and circuit boards I couldn't name.

I turned and headed back into the hallway. The sound—whatever it was—had died away now. I held my breath and listened for it again, but there was nothing. I made a cautious descent down into the dining room and the kitchen beyond.

The door to the basement was still ajar from when I'd slammed it open hauling Alissa up the stairs.

That seemed like an eternity ago.

I made my way back down the stairs and now I could hear the mechanical sounds again, the squeak and thrum of wheels, gears, and timing belts, or so I imagined.

I alighted onto the basement's cement floor. The rope Alissa used to hang herself still swung from the rafters above me; I shuddered and moved past it, eager to put it behind me.

In front of me, the room grew considerably colder, although I sensed it had nothing to do with the fact I was underground. That chill felt like a curtain, a

wall of invisible mist I had to step through to get to the machine on the workbench in front of me.

There was a laptop there, hooked up to something bigger and boxy by a web of wires, but the actual technology looked out of place alongside it: it looked like an old reel-to-reel tape recorder. A little further down the workbench was a longer plastic box, maybe a foot tall, set on one end. As I watched, a shutter in the side of the box opened and a beam of white light, maybe the width of a pencil, shot out and splashed itself across the reel-to-reel looking device.

Again, there was the odd keening sound, but now it seemed to come from everywhere at once: from the very walls of the basement itself, invisible in the dimness down here. I could all but feel that noise, the vibrations raising goosebumps on my forearms as I took a step closer toward the machinery and the laptop on the work bench.

The laptop seemed bright in the dim light. I had to blink before I could read what the screen said.

The lines on the screen were numbered, 1 through 13. I swallowed hard, mouth dry.

I read the same phrase on each of those thirteen lines: "Vince Welch did not kill me."

Thirteen lines, I thought.

One for each of Vince Welch's supposed victims.

Idaho had killed an innocent man.

Tommie Simmons grew up in the Denver, Colorado area and worked as a reporter covering crime and courts, first in Northern Colorado and then in Boise, Idaho. He is currently in his third year of law school, interested in working in criminal defense.

More From Undertaker Books

Purchase at UndertakerBooks.com and other online retailers

Ink Vine

Elizabeth Broadbent

Shadows of Appalachia

D.L. Winchester

The Taste of Women

Cyan LeBlanc

Mastering The Art of Female Cookery

Cyan LeBlanc

In Memory of Exoskeltons

Rebecca Cuthbert

Stories To Take To Your Grave: Vol. 1

(Anthology)

A Terrible Place and Other Flashes of Darkness

D.L. Winchester

The Triangle + The Deep Double Feature

Robert P. Ottone

Silent Mine

C.M. Saunders

Odd Jobs: Six Files from the Department of Inhuman Resources

(Anthology)

Undertaker Books

www.undertakerbooks.com

If you are a fan of horror stories and tales,
you'll want to follow Undertaker Books.

We're bringing you stories to take to your grave.

SIGN UP FOR OUR NEWSLETTER ONLINE

www.ingramcontent.com/pod-product-compliance
Lightning Source LLC
Chambersburg PA
CBHW060453300726

48975CB00008B/2496